To Phoe

BRONTË
TEMPESTRA
AND THE
ICE WARRIORS

Stay!
cool!

B Blog x

The Bronte Tempestra series

Look out for more

BRONTE TEMPESTRA

AND THE
ICE WARRIORS

BEX HOGAN
Illustrated by Hannah McCaffery

First published in Great Britain in 2024 by

PICCADILLY PRESS

4th Floor, Victoria House, Bloomsbury Square

London WC1B 4DA

Owned by Bonnier Books

Sveavägen 56, Stockholm, Sweden

bonnierbooks.co.uk/PiccadillyPress

A CIP catalogue record for this book is available from the British Library.

ISBN: 978-1-80078-492-5

Also available as an ebook and in audio

1

Typeset by Emily Bornoff

Printed and bound in Great Britain by Clays Ltd, Elcograf S.p.A.

Piccadilly Press is an imprint of Bonnier Books UK

bonnierbooks.co.uk

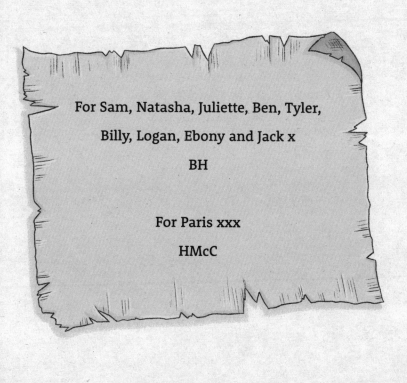

For Sam, Natasha, Juliette, Ben, Tyler,

Billy, Logan, Ebony and Jack x

BH

For Paris xxx

HMcC

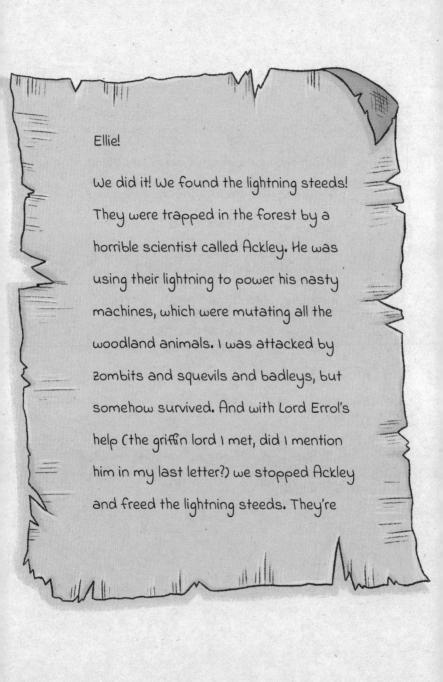

Ellie!

We did it! We found the lightning steeds! They were trapped in the forest by a horrible scientist called Ackley. He was using their lightning to power his nasty machines, which were mutating all the woodland animals. I was attacked by zombits and squevils and badleys, but somehow survived. And with Lord Errol's help (the griffin lord I met, did I mention him in my last letter?) we stopped Ackley and freed the lightning steeds. They're

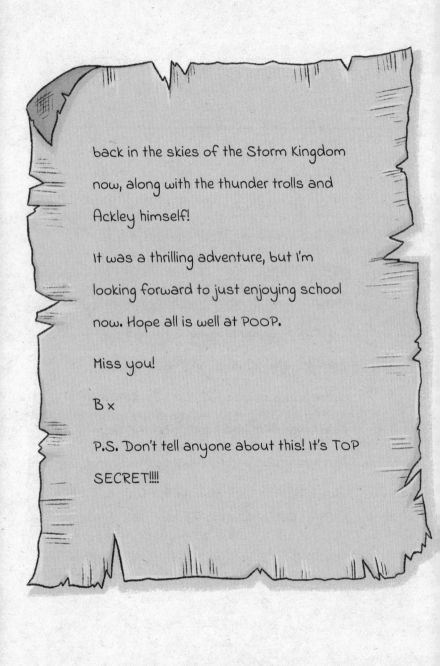

back in the skies of the Storm Kingdom now, along with the thunder trolls and Ackley himself!

It was a thrilling adventure, but I'm looking forward to just enjoying school now. Hope all is well at POOP.

Miss you!

B x

P.S. Don't tell anyone about this! It's TOP SECRET!!!!

School Diary, Day 64

Can't believe how fast this first term is going. A small part of the forest has been declared safe and it's been fun to do Forest Care classes and not have the creatures trying to eat me! Lady Fennel is doing an amazing job de-monstering them. But I miss her. Hope she comes back soon.

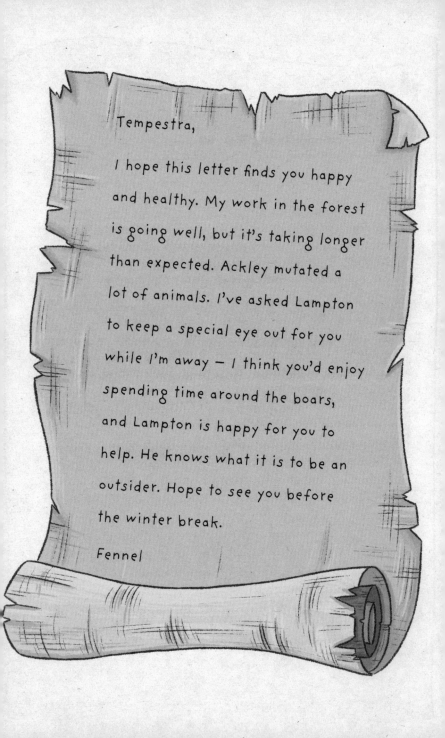

Tempestra,

I hope this letter finds you happy and healthy. My work in the forest is going well, but it's taking longer than expected. Ackley mutated a lot of animals. I've asked Lampton to keep a special eye out for you while I'm away — I think you'd enjoy spending time around the boars, and Lampton is happy for you to help. He knows what it is to be an outsider. Hope to see you before the winter break.

Fennel

KNIGHTS WEEKLY

The annual Welcome Winter jousting tournament took place this weekend, and has given us a new champion! Sir Montford Mallow, rising star of the tournaments, has beaten the previous record held for many years by Sir Roland Ripple.

Asked how he felt about his victory, Sir Mallow said, 'I've always known I was capable of becoming the best knight ever. It's no surprise at all to me that I've not only won, but smashed all previous records.' Sir Ripple was not available for comment.

The Mighty Montford Mallow

REALMS' ROUND-UP

SCHOOL STAFFING SHENANIGANS?

Rumour has it that all is not well at Sir Sebastian's School for Squires. First, there was the sudden retirement of headmaster Sir Percival Blake, only days into the new term. And now, according to one disgruntled parent, there aren't enough teachers at all!

We hear that Sir Blake's replacement, Sir Calliphus, spends all his time up in his tower, presumably doing whatever it is that headmasters do, while newly appointed Lady Fennel went on temporary leave less than a week after starting her post.

'That's what you get for hiring a woman,' the unhappy parent said. 'Not up to the task.'

He also reported that his son was told the arrival of new staff had been delayed due to the damage caused by the thunder trolls' recent rampage. But this parent is sceptical.

'It's all gone downhill since they let girls in,' he said. 'My son is in the same class as one and she's been nothing but trouble.'

We reached out to Sir Sebastian's for comment and were told, 'Absolutely everything is fine.'

B!!

I can't believe it's only a few more weeks until the winter break! I'm so looking forward to visiting the Snow Kingdom with my family. We're going to do everything snowy I can think of— snow angels, frozen bubble bashing, and building the biggest snowman ever made. We're going to stay in a snow cottage and I'm going to do all the snow sports. Blizzard ball, ice-cave diving, frost-owl sky races — everything! Plus, I'm hoping we might even be allowed to go and see the famous ice thistle. Wouldn't that be magical?

Enjoy the rest of term,
El x

Cabbages

Bronte Tempestra crept silently towards her target. Her mission was simple: capture the villain. Her breath coiled in the cold air, slithering like a mist-snake before disappearing. She raised her weapon slowly. She must not be seen. That was essential to her success.

She could imagine the glory already! How, after she'd saved the school, everyone would cheer! The teachers would proclaim a half-day holiday in her honour and the students would be so grateful they'd buy her presents and offer to do her chores, while the headmaster would award her a special commendation for exceptional bravery!

Bronte leaped forward, striking with her weapon and ... **SQUELCH!**

She fell face first into the mud.

'Oh feathers,' she groaned, dripping sludge as she sat up.

The villain grunted loudly, as if he was laughing, and Bronte narrowed her eyes.

'Yeah, yeah, very funny,' she said to the tufty pigling. 'But I'll catch you eventually.'

She retrieved her weapon – in this case, a harness – and shook off the worst of the mud. There would be no heroic celebrations for her today.

'He is such a *nightmare*!' Bronte said, looking

over at Blue, her icekitten, who was wisely keeping well away from the mud. 'Honestly, how many times has he escaped now?'

Blue huffed a puff of ice.

'Exactly,' Bronte said. 'Too many.'

Despite it being Sunday, Bronte had woken early in a futile attempt to catch up with some of her homework, but before she had even begun to write her essay (*Hobgoblins: Friend or Foe?*) she'd caught sight of the fiendish boar trampling through the vegetable gardens.

The battle boars at Sir Sebastian's were mainly fed clouds, but they really would eat anything. Ice, seaweed, prickles, sapphires, mudroot – *anything*! Pig was no exception, and he was also incredibly greedy. Vegetables might be waaaay down his list of favourites, but they were still food.

Bronte had felt certain she could catch Pig and return him to the pens before he ate *all* the vegetables, and so had hurried out into the chilly winter morning. But Pig clearly had no intention of being deprived of his very big breakfast.

'Honestly, you'd think you'd be nicer to me, after I saved your life,' Bronte said to him, as she trudged across the field. 'If it weren't for me and Blue, you'd be one of Ackley's monsters, and I'm certain he wouldn't be feeding you treats.'

Bronte drew closer to where Pig was munching a very large mouthful of carrots and parsnips.

'If you come with me,' she said, 'I'll bring you some leftovers from dinner. Crispy vine leaves stuffed with sweet paste and berries.'

Pig eyed her suspiciously, chewing slowly. Bronte crept closer.

'And if you're very good, I'll crush some ice

cubes on top like sprinkles . . .' she promised in a
sing-song voice.

It was enough. Pig allowed her to slip the
rope halter over his tusks and around his head.
Crushed ice was his absolute favourite.

'See?' Bronte asked, breathing a sigh of relief.
'Was that so bad?'

Pig replied with a massive
buuuurrrPPPPP!

'Charming,' Bronte groaned. Boar belches
stank!

'Come on,' she said to Pig and Blue.

But they had only taken a few steps before
Pig squealed loudly and bolted – stampeding
through the vegetable patch and dragging
Bronte behind him!

'Whooooahhhhhh!' Bronte cried, still clinging
to the end of the rope.

'What are you two doing?' A stern voice stopped Pig in his tracks and Bronte looked up, blinking the mud from her eyes. Lampton, who was in charge of the battle boars, was doing his best to look cross, but was struggling to hide his smile.

'Pig escaped again,' Bronte said, scrambling to her feet, and noticing that Blue was running towards the boar pens, leaving her to deal with this mess alone.

'So I see. At least he didn't break into the cloud shed this time and eat all the supplies.' Lampton sighed. 'What are we going to do with you?' he asked, scratching the pigling's whiskery snout.

Pig simply snorted.

'It's these sparkly tusks of yours,' Lampton said. 'Ever since you got them, you've broken through every door and fence.' He glanced at

Bronte. 'How *did* he get them, do you think?'

Bronte blushed and stared at the ground.

Only weeks ago, when she had first started at Sir Sebastian's School for Squires, Bronte had uncovered a dastardly scheme in the old forest, where a scientist named Ackley had been mutating all the woodland animals into monsters. He'd hoped to attack the two schools for royalty in the Realm of Education – the Palace for Obedient and Outstanding Princesses (POOP) and the School for Independent and Courageous Kings (SICK) – as his first step to reclaiming the throne of the Oak Kingdom.

The headmaster, Sir Blake, had allowed it to happen, and then retired in disgrace. His replacement, Sir Calliphus, had decided to keep the whole situation a secret for the sake of the school's reputation, and so he'd instructed Bronte never to speak of what had happened. The only other people who knew were Bronte's best friends, Tonkins and Ellie, and her favourite teacher, Lady Fennel. Oh, and Lord Errol of the First Battalion of Griffins.

Sir Calliphus had explained Pig's new dazzling tusks away with a sweep of his arm, muttering, 'That sometimes happens.'

Lampton clearly didn't believe him, however. He'd already tried to coax the truth from Bronte several times. She wished she could tell him about how Pig had been mutated, and that although the changes had been reversed, the diamond tusks had stayed. She felt certain Lampton could be trusted. But she didn't want to get into trouble with Sir Calliphus.

Lampton sighed. 'I'll be fixing his pen today, then. Could you help me muck out?'

Bronte hesitated. She really needed to finish that essay, but she enjoyed helping Lampton. 'Can I change first?' she asked with a smile.

'If you want, but you'll only get dirty again. Oh, and you'd better go and tell Chef what's happened,' Lampton said rather apologetically. 'Warn him only the cabbages have survived.'

Great, Bronte thought as she traipsed back towards her treehouse. *Cabbages for tea. Not even Pig had wanted to eat* them!

New Arrivals

After Bronte had changed and visited the kitchens (Chef was *not* happy about the cabbage situation), she headed back to the boar pens.

She was trying not to worry about her essay, or the family tree project she had to finish. Having only started Sir Sebastian's earlier that term, Bronte was still making up for lost time, and if she didn't pass her exams at the end of the school year, she wouldn't be able to move up from Year Four to Year Five. Her parents would probably make her go back to POOP if that happened and that was *not* an option. She still had a lot of homework to do and there was only a week left before the break for winter festivities.

Everyone else seemed so excited to go home, and while Bronte was looking forward to seeing her family, part of her wished she could stay at Sir Sebastian's. It had taken her a while to settle in, and now that she had, she didn't want to leave.

Lampton was hard at work repairing the broken fence of Pig's pen, and smiled at Bronte as she arrived.

'Where's Blue?' Bronte asked, looking around for her icekitten who had abandoned her so unceremoniously.

'Oh, he was here a minute ago,' Lampton replied, pausing briefly in his work.

'He's been wandering off a lot recently,' Bronte

said with a sigh. 'I have no idea where he keeps going.'

'Maybe he's exploring the secret tunnels beneath the school,' Lampton said with a grin.

'The *what*?'

'I'm only teasing,' Lampton said. 'It's just a story my old dad used to tell me. He worked here before me, and his father before him. Used to tell all sorts of made-up legends and myths about this place.'

'Such as?' Bronte asked, fascinated. She loved stories!

'Let's see if I can remember,' Lampton said, scratching his head. 'Oh yes, that long before the school was built, back when this land was still part of the old Tree Kingdoms, whole villages lived below the ground in tunnels supported by the tree roots. The story goes that the first headmaster ordered they be left there and kept secret, so he could hide in them if the school was ever under attack!'

'Why would a knight want to hide?' Bronte asked, before remembering how reluctant the knights seemed to be to face danger of any kind.

'My favourite part of the story was about the glow-crawlers. Strange creatures who lived beneath the school and had a reputation for being very slow.'

'Oh, wouldn't it be wonderful if they were real!' Bronte sighed, and Lampton chuckled.

'Well, if they are, I've never seen them. Don't worry about Blue – he'll turn up again soon.'

But there was no sign of the icekitten while Bronte worked. It was only after she'd finished scrubbing out the boar pens and was tipping her final load of poop onto the muck heap that

Bronte caught sight of a familiar flash of blue.
She left the wheelbarrow and went to investigate.

At the edge of the field, where the muck heap
hit the hedge, she found her icekitten with his
head in a hole and bottom in the air!

'Blue! What are you doing?' Bronte asked.
'You'd better not have been rolling in poop or I'll
have to bath you before you come anywhere near
my bed.'

But Blue didn't even look up at the sound of her voice.

'What have you found? Are you hunting mislets?' The small rodents that lived in the hedgerows were one of Blue's favourite snacks.

Blue wiggled out of the hole and puffed a little ice from his nose to clear the dirt. He jumped up and down excitedly, eager for Bronte to look.

'OK,' she agreed. 'It's not like I could get any dirtier today. Have you found a way into Lampton's secret tunnels?'

'Bronts!'

Bronte turned to see Tonkins running up the hill, panting hard, with his firecat Dotty easily keeping pace beside him. She waved to them.

'There you are!' Tonkins said. 'I've been looking all over for you. Where've you been all day?'

'It's a long story,' she said. 'But blame Pig.'

'OK, well tell me later, because right now, you have to come with me.'

'Why, what's wrong?' Bronte said, forgetting about the hole and hurrying towards him.

'Nothing. They're here. The new teachers are here!'

Bronte gasped with excitement, and together the two friends ran back towards the school, with Blue and Dotty just behind them.

Since all the drama in the forest, the school had been short of teachers. Sir Calliphus had replaced Sir Blake as headteacher, and so didn't have as much time to be in the classroom. And Lady Fennel had left to reverse the mutations on the forest animals, and still hadn't come back. Sir Ripple had taken most of their lessons since, so new teachers were an exciting prospect.

They should have arrived *ages* ago, but couldn't because of the travel chaos caused by the thunder trolls' destruction.

Bronte and Tonkins ran into the courtyard, where other students had already formed a crowd, all keen to see the newcomers. Tonkins jumped up and down to try to see over the taller students, but Bronte grabbed his arm and pulled him with her as she wound her way to the front.

Sir Calliphus was waiting at the gates to welcome the new arrivals.

'How many do you think there will be?' Bronte asked Tonkins, raising her voice over the surrounding chatter.

Tonkins shrugged. 'Dunno. It would be nice to have some different teachers, wouldn't it? Apart from Lady Fennel it's been the same old people for years. Higgins Boseley said he heard that a knight from the Rose Kingdom was coming, but then Connor Devlan said that *he* heard there were twin knights coming from the Fire Kingdom, and Felix Collins said that *he'd* heard a rumour that…'

He trailed off, his mouth opening and shutting but no sound coming out. And then:

'No way. *No way!* Bronts, LOOK!!!'

Bronte followed his gaze and watched as a young man stepped out of the carriage to shake hands with Sir Calliphus. He was wearing tight leather trousers and a white shirt with a chainmail waistcoat. The hat he wore was wide brimmed, with a point at the front, much like Lord Errol's beak. When he pulled it off to tuck it under his arm, his slick chestnut hair remained perfectly in place. He wore an expression of total smugness and Bronte couldn't help but roll her eyes.

Tonkins was positively shaking with excitement and clung onto Bronte's sleeve.

'That's ... that's ... Sir Montford Mallow!'

'Who?' Bronte asked, guessing from the reaction of everyone else that she was the only clueless one there.

'You know how Sir Ripple always goes on about being a former cover model for *Knights Weekly*? Well Sir Mallow is the current front cover knight. He's amazing! I can't believe he's here!' Tonkins gasped. 'What if he teaches us? How will I ever cope with being in his presence? I mean *look at him*. He's a legend!'

Bronte glanced back at Sir Mallow, who was now walking with a swagger into the courtyard, waving at the delighted students. His cream-and-chestnut-striped firecat had a strut to match.

Just as they were about to pass Bronte and
Tonkins, Blue let out a huge sneeze. All the dirt he
had breathed in while
burrowing into the
hole flew out –
as well as a
blast of ice.
Bronte
gasped as Sir
Mallow
stepped
onto the
slippery
ground, instantly
sliding forward and
wobbling frantically to keep
his balance.

The crowd fell silent in shock, and when he

didn't fall, the students burst into applause at his recovery. But the knight was searching for the culprit. His gaze fell on Blue, who slunk behind Bronte's legs. Sir Mallow narrowed his eyes. Then, as if remembering everyone was looking, Sir Mallow swiftly swapped his glare for a grin. He waved once more while his firecat melted the ice patch. One boy ran out in front of Sir Mallow with a quill and scroll, and the knight happily scrawled his autograph. That was all the permission everyone else needed. They swooped on him like a flock of birds, calling his name and begging him to sign their parchments, their clothes – even their skin!

Tonkins cast around desperately. 'Bronts, have you got a quill on you?'

She raised her eyebrows. 'I'm covered in boar poop. Why would I have a quill?'

'Right. Wait there. I've got to go and get one!'
And Tonkins darted off towards the triple-trunk
oak tree where their treehouses were.

Bronte chuckled to herself and turned back to
see who else was appearing from the carriage.

Another older knight had already climbed out
and was talking animatedly with Sir Calliphus.
But Bronte wasn't paying much attention to
them. Because stepping down from the carriage
was a woman. She didn't appear to be a warrior
like Lady Fennel. Her thick velvet cloak was
wrapped around her as she looked up at the
school and smiled.

She looked nice, Bronte thought, and she
crossed her fingers, hoping she might have
the new teacher for some lessons. The cloaked
woman was soon joined by another knight and
Sir Calliphus escorted the group towards school.

So there they were, the new teachers. It was definitely shaping up to be an interesting last week of term. Bronte just hoped that none of them set her any more homework!

Roommates

Bronte woke slowly the next morning. She was warm and cosy, wrapped in her blanket. She had been dreaming of the winter festivities back home, of the yummy food and all the presents. Winter in the Storm Kingdom meant extra lightning and thunder, and the thunder trolls would knock loose the icy clouds, which floated down to the kingdom below like snowflakes. She could almost imagine it now. Blue happily rolling in the carpet of cloudy softness –

'Morning!'

Bronte screamed as she sat up, almost falling out of her hammock.

There was another girl in her room, smiling at Bronte as she opened the curtains. She was older than Bronte, and taller too, with a no-nonsense air about her. Her hair was short with tight brown curls that bounced whenever she moved her head.

'Sorry, didn't mean to scare you,' the girl said with a slightly mischievous grin. 'I arrived really late last night and didn't want to disturb you. I'm Nix.'

'Hi,' Bronte said. 'I'm –'

'Oh, I know who you are, Stormy,' Nix said, the grin widening. 'Apparently you're the reason we all had cabbage soup for dinner last night. Chef was still grumbling as he heated some up for me when I arrived – he really wasn't happy.'

'It wasn't my fault!' Bronte cried, but Nix laughed.

'I'm only teasing you,' she said. 'Relax.'

Bronte still felt as if she were half asleep, and rubbed her eyes. 'So, did you arrive with the new teachers yesterday?'

'Nah, I came later. I'm not even here officially. I go to the trade skills school in the Realm of Education. You know, the First Academy of Royal Trades?'

Before Bronte could say anything, Nix quickly added, 'I know, I know, who wants to go to a school known as FART, right? But that's not why I'm here. My parents make armour, but I've always wanted to wear it rather than make it, so they said I could come here for a taster. If I like it, I can swap schools next term.'

'Oh, breezy,' Bronte said. It would be really nice to have someone to share the treehouse with. 'What year are you in?'

'Seven,' Nix said. 'So I would be reeeeeeally behind. That's the thing.'

Bronte knew what that felt like. She'd rushed to finish her hobgoblin essay before bed and it was far from her best work.

'Well I hope you like it here,' Bronte said, hopping out of her hammock and stretching. Blue was stirring now too, and sniffing Nix suspiciously.

'Is this your firecat?' Nix asked, bending down to scratch Blue's chin.

'Yep, well he's an icekitten, actually.'

'So cute!' Nix said. 'Oh, he has a muddy nose.'

'Yeah, he keeps digging holes up near the muck heap.'

'Lovely!' Nix laughed, moving away from Blue, who snorted a flurry of ice at her feet in response. 'Hey,' she said, gesturing to the knitted toy Bronte was clutching. 'Is that supposed to be Sir Pen Tine?'

Bronte blushed. 'Um, yeah.'

'I love it,' Nix said. 'Always loved those stories. Spent years pretending to slay the Swirklebirkle! Anyhoo, I'm starving – I'm gonna go grab some breakfast. You coming?'

Bronte beamed at the new girl. A fellow Sir Pen Tine fan? They were going to get on splendidly! 'You go,' Bronte said. 'I need to get dressed.'

'OK, see you later,' Nix said, heading to the doorway. But when she opened it, a burst of icy air blasted into the treehouse. 'What the – Hey, Stormy, it's snowing!'

Bronte ran to peer outside and gasped.

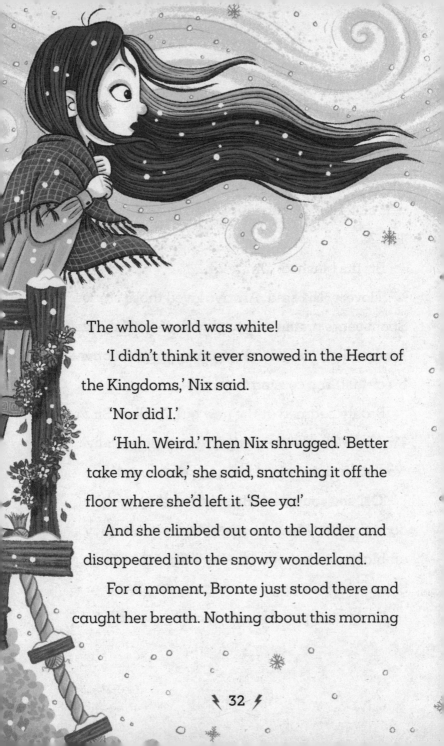

The whole world was white!

'I didn't think it ever snowed in the Heart of the Kingdoms,' Nix said.

'Nor did I.'

'Huh. Weird.' Then Nix shrugged. 'Better take my cloak,' she said, snatching it off the floor where she'd left it. 'See ya!'

And she climbed out onto the ladder and disappeared into the snowy wonderland.

For a moment, Bronte just stood there and caught her breath. Nothing about this morning

had been what she'd expected! A new roommate,
and *snow*? Then she hurried to pull on her clothes
so she didn't freeze on the way to the bathroom
block.

Once she was washed and properly dressed,
Bronte hurried to the dining hall, eager to talk
to Tonkins. Blue chose to stay outside, enjoying
leaping and diving into the deep snow.

The firecats were not so excited, all huddling
under the dining tables and shivering. Bronte
looked around for Tonkins, but she couldn't see

him anywhere. Usually he was easily spotted by his floppy wide-brimmed hat with a massive red feather. She was just about to sit on the empty end of a table, when she saw someone waving at her.

'Bronts, over here!'

Tonkins? Her friend was virtually unrecognisable, wearing trousers that looked several sizes too small, and a waistcoat that seemed to be a jacket with the sleeves messily cut off. And his trademark hat was gone, replaced with one that looked suspiciously like Sir Mallow's. Bronte gave him an uncertain smile as she sat down. 'Nice hat,' she teased.

Tonkins didn't notice the tone. 'Isn't it great? Bobby Watson had a spare one and he gave it to me. Well, I had to give him a month's allowance, but it's totally worth it, right? I think it suits me better than the old one. It's a bit more sophisticated, I think – frames my face. That's important, you know. I read it in *Knights Weekly*.'

'If you say so,' Bronte replied dubiously. 'Hey, listen, I didn't know it snowed down here.'

Tonkins shrugged, taking a bite of his ten-high stack of pancakes. At least there was no cabbage for breakfast, Bronte noticed with relief.

'It doesn't often,' he said. 'But hopefully it'll mean no lessons.'

Moments later, Tonkins had that hope crushed as prefects started passing out scrolls.

'What's this?' Tonkins asked through a mouthful of food.

'New timetables. Just for this week,' the prefect said. 'Because of the new teachers.'

Bronte unrolled the scroll and held it flat on the table so she and Tonkins could read it.

And then Tonkins practically choked on his pancakes, so that Bronte had to hastily pat him on the back.

'It's happening!' he cried. 'Look, Bronts. We've got lessons with Sir Mallow!'

'Right now as well,' Bronte said, her mood dropping as fast as Tonkins's was rising. After the way Blue had caused Sir Mallow to slip, she didn't imagine he would be pleased to see her.

'Then hurry up!' Tonkins said, and shot to his feet. 'We can't be late!'

Sir Mallow

The snow was still falling as they made their way to the armoury. Their first lesson was Armour Care with Sir Mallow, and Bronte thought that Tonkins might actually burst with excitement.

While most of the students were enjoying the unexpected snowfall, Bronte couldn't help feeling a bit worried about it. Maybe it was because the last time the weather here had been unusual, it was the start of all sorts of problems. And Bronte just wanted to enjoy the rest of her first term before she had to go home. Absolutely no trouble allowed!

A snowball hit her on the back between her shoulder blades. Bronte spun round to see Lance and his buddies, Leo and Pole, laughing and preparing to fire another one at Tonkins.

Bronte snatched Tonkins's new hat from his head just in time to use it as a shield to protect him – the snowball splattered into it, leaving

behind melting white flakes.

'Don't ruin my hat!' Tonkins said, yanking
it back from her. 'I want to make a good first
impression with Sir Mallow.'

'Sorry,' she said, surprised. She had thought
Tonkins would be impressed by her quick
thinking and cool catch. Not to mention stopping
Lance from hitting him. She followed him into the
armoury, more than a little confused.

They sat down on the floor but there was no sign of Sir Mallow, much to Tonkins's obvious disappointment.

'Welcome, young squires, to another week of learning.' Sir Ripple strode into the room. 'Your last week, in fact, before the winter festivities. Assuming you actually make it home in this atrocious weather!'

He continued to ramble on, but Bronte was stuck on those last words. There was a chance they could be snowed in? Breezy! Maybe the snow wasn't such a bad thing after all.

'Excuse me, sir, but isn't Sir Mallow supposed to be teaching us?' Tonkins asked.

'He is.' Sir Ripple sounded annoyed. 'I have simply come to make an introduction, but our new teacher seems to have got lost on the way here.'

There was a collective groan, and Sir Ripple's face fell.

'We can make do perfectly well on our own. Now, as you know, I pride myself on having gleaming armour,' Sir Ripple continued. 'Because after all, first impressions are everything. If a princess were to require rescuing, would she want a knight in dirty armour, or one who dazzled?'

One who was competent would be nice, Bronte thought to herself.

'So today, we're going to practise buffing up those breast plates! Lance, could you hand out these cloths?'

Lance reluctantly did as he was told, chucking the grimiest ones he could find at Bronte and Tonkins.

But before they could start polishing, the door to the armoury burst open.

'Put down your rags, children!' Sir Mallow said, striking a power pose, a helmet under his arm. 'I have arranged something far more exciting. Come outside and see.'

Sir Ripple visibly bristled at the sight of the younger knight. 'You are late, sir. And I don't think that's appropriate –'

But the rest of his words were drowned out by the excited students leaping up and hurrying out into the snow.

Bronte offered Sir Ripple an apologetic smile as she followed the rest of the class.

Blue came bounding happily over to her, his fur wet from diving through snow. The firecats still looked miserable though, puffing fire at the offending white stuff and trying to melt it away.

Sir Mallow was standing by a massive block of ice, as tall as he was. Lampton was tipping a second block off his old wheelbarrow, and he did not look pleased.

'The boar troughs were frozen solid this morning and, when I heard, I knew exactly what to do with the ice blocks,' said Sir Mallow with a flourish. 'Naturally, I am quite the sculpting expert. I thought you might like a demonstration.'

'And then can we have a go, sir?' Varney asked excitedly.

Sir Mallow hesitated. 'If there's time.'

Sir Ripple strode out, to stand beside the other ice block. 'I think you'll find *I* am the superior sculptor and therefore should be the one to demonstrate.'

'Well, you were once the poster boy for *Knights Weekly*, but things change,' Sir Mallow shot back. Their two firecats circled each other suspiciously, hissing and spitting sparks of fire.

'Good luck,' Lampton muttered to the class as he took the wheelbarrow away.

The two teachers selected a tool – Lampton had brought axes, chisels and mallets – and got to work. They hacked and chipped away at the ice, shooting each other deadly, competitive looks.

'Is this something they do at tournaments?' Bronte asked Tonkins, in confusion.

'Yeah, in the winter. They paint in the summer tournaments, make floral sculptures in the spring and mould clay in the autumn. Self-portraits are an important skill for a knight, you know.'

Of course they were. Bronte sighed. She still forgot sometimes how much the knights cared about tournaments and looking good. But it was fun to watch the two knights at work – at first, anyway.

As the lesson dragged on, with no end to the demonstration in sight, Bronte was growing increasingly cold and soggy. She could barely feel her fingers or toes, and desperately wanted to move around rather than just standing still. Despite the fact that Lampton had brought up several more ice blocks, it was clear there would be no time for the students to practise *their* skills. Still, Bronte suspected the boys would have happily turned to ice statues themselves if it meant they got to watch Sir Mallow for a little while longer.

The firecats had retreated into the armoury, but Blue was having the time of his life, scampering back and forth between the two ice sculptures and turning somersaults in the snow. As Sir Ripple chipped furiously to define his statue's jawline, he sent a flurry of ice flakes into the air. Blue leaped up, wanting to catch them on his tongue.

'Get away!' Sir Ripple cried, raising his arm protectively between the icekitten and his masterpiece.

Sir Mallow glanced up and laughed to see Sir Ripple's distress, but then his expression turned thunderous at the sight of Blue. 'Hey, I recognise him!'

Bronte hurried over, deciding it was best to intervene before Blue caused more chaos.

But Sir Ripple was waving his arms at the oblivious icekitten, and as Bronte stretched out to reach Blue, Sir Ripple hit her straight in the face.

'**OW!**' she cried, her hands flying to her nose. That had really hurt!

Sir Ripple gasped in horror. 'My apologies, young squire!' And then he saw the blood trailing down Bronte's face. 'Don't panic, don't panic,' he said, panicking. 'Tonkins, take her to the nurse.'

Tonkins frowned. 'We have a nurse?'

'Yes, delightful woman. She arrived with me yesterday,' Sir Mallow said. 'In fact, she was the one who mentioned she'd noticed the frozen troughs on her walk this morning. Now, do be a good lad, and run this girl along to the herbery, before she bleeds on our sculptures.'

Tonkins's face went pale as he gazed at Sir Mallow. When he didn't move, frozen in adoration, Bronte groaned and tugged his sleeve, calling Blue to follow.

When they were out of earshot, Tonkins gave a strange little squeak.

'He talked to me, Bronts! Sir Mallow! He knows I exist!'

'I'm happy for you,' Bronte said, her voice

sounding silly as she pinched her bleeding nose, 'but don't you think he's a bit full of himself?'

'He's the coolest knight in the whole of the kingdoms!' Tonkins breathed. 'He's allowed to be.'

'OK, if you say so,' Bronte said. 'Listen, I'm fine, so if you want to go back, you can. I don't want you missing your Mallow-time for no reason.'

'You sure?' Tonkins asked, but he was already stepping away. 'You're the best, Bronts, thanks. I'll see you later!'

Miss Shine

Bronte smiled before swiftly wincing at the pain in her nose. She had never seen Tonkins like this before. But then, she supposed meeting your real-life hero must be pretty breezy. She imagined how it would feel if Sir Pen Tine were actually real, and then turned up to start teaching here . . . Yep, she would definitely be star-struck!

And she really was fine – a little gentle prodding of her nose suggested it was only a bit bruised. She was more than able to visit the nurse on her own. In all the weeks since she'd started at Sir Sebastian's, Bronte had never been to the herbery. Medicinal lessons didn't start until Year Six, something Bronte was sad about. But she supposed it was nice to have new things to look forward to.

As they walked, Blue was blasting the snow and sliding on the ice he'd made. Bronte couldn't help but smile, despite the stingy pain.

'I'm glad you're having a good time,' she said, amused by how oblivious Blue was to the chaos he was causing. This weather really was made for him. She, on the other hand, would need to put on some warmer clothes if she wanted to play in the snow with him later.

Bronte was frozen through by the time she reached the herbery, and she shivered as she went inside.

Even with her bloodied nose, she couldn't help but inhale the room's scent – it smelled like gardens and summer. Hundreds of bottles and jars lined the shelves, all filled with dried leaves and flowers. At the work bench stood the woman Bronte had seen arrive with Sir Mallow. Her dress was thick maroon velvet, and her long dark hair was loose down her back as she crushed something to powder with her pestle and mortar.

When she heard Bronte come in, she looked up and smiled. It was one of those smiles that made a whole face light up.

'Hello,' she said. 'Oh dear, what happened to you?'

'Sir Ripple and Sir Mallow were ice sculpting,'

Bronte said, feeling it was as good an explanation as any.

The woman smiled. 'Ah. I fear that might be my fault. Let's have a look then.' And she walked up to Bronte and removed her hands from her nose.

'It's already stopped bleeding, so you'll be fine,' the woman said. 'Let me get you some ice to make sure it doesn't swell up.'

The woman took a piece of clean cloth and went outside. Moments later she returned and pressed the ice pack gently against Bronte's nose.

Bronte sighed with relief as the pain subsided.

'The snow has its uses,' the woman said. 'Leave that on for a few minutes before you go back to class. Here, have a seat.'

She pulled out a stool for Bronte to perch on.

'I'm Miss Shine. And you are?'

'Bronte Tempestra.'

'Ah, yes, the storm princess,' Miss Shine said. 'I've heard all about you.'

Bronte's eyes widened in alarm and Miss Shine laughed.

'Don't worry, nothing bad,' she said, before adding, 'well, nothing *too* bad.' The twinkle in her eye reassured Bronte that she was just joking.

'Are you from the Sun Kingdom?' Bronte asked, desperate to change the subject.

'I can see why you might think that, given my name, but no. I'm from all over. Never settled anywhere for too long.'

'Will you stay here then?'

'We'll see,' Miss Shine said. 'I'm happy to teach for a while.'

'Oh! You're teaching? I thought you were the nurse,' Bronte said, confused.

'I'm a bit of everything,' Miss Shine said. 'In fact, I'm teaching you later today, I believe. Chivalry class.'

A teacher who hadn't been on the cover of *Knights Weekly*? That would make a nice change, Bronte thought.

'But first, I need to finish preparing the herbs for a medicinal lesson. Why don't you close your eyes and relax for a few minutes?'

Bronte did as she was told, and despite all her insistence she was fine, she welcomed the rest.

Once Miss Shine was happy that Bronte was fully recovered, Bronte returned to her class. Sir Mallow's sculpture was almost finished and definitely bore a stronger resemblance to him than Sir Ripple's did, but after catching a glimpse of poor Sir Ripple looking dejected, Bronte thought it best not to say anything.

Tonkins was still beaming in delight that Sir Mallow had spoken to him, and carried on beaming long after the lesson was over. As he and Bronte made their way to Calligraphy, Tonkins talked endlessly about how amazing Sir Mallow was. He continued to do so all through the lesson too, even while Bronte tried to focus on her work.

He carried on his Sir Mallow adoration as they walked to Chivalry class. They passed Sir Mallow and Sir Ripple, still out in the courtyard, chiselling away at another ice block each with another class held captive. How many ice statues did one school need?

Tonkins probably would have carried on singing Sir Mallow's praises during Chivalry class too, but Miss Shine immediately set them a problem to solve.

'Right, Year Four, consider this,' Miss Shine said. 'You come upon a burning tower, and trapped inside is a princess. How might you rescue her? Lance?'

Lance shrugged. 'Tell her to jump and catch her?'

'You just got yourself a splatted princess because you missed. Anyone else? Yes, Higgles?'

'Shoot an arrow in through her window with a rope attached, and then climb up it?'

'You just shot your princess through the chest, because the smoke blocked your view.'

Tonkins raised his hand and leaped to his feet. 'I would greet the princess with a bow,' he said, demonstrating flamboyantly. 'I would introduce myself, and declare my good intentions to rescue her. And then I would scale the tower wall, climbing the ivy, pull myself in through the window, kiss the princess's hand, and then offer to carry her back down to safety.'

Miss Shine smiled. 'Alas, Tonkins, there is no ivy on this tower. Not that it would matter, because your princess would already have died from smoke inhalation while you were busy faffing about.'

The class laughed and Tonkins sat back down, rather sulkily. Bronte patted his arm, though she too couldn't help but grin.

'Bronte, how about you?' Miss Shine asked. 'Since you're a princess, perhaps you'll have a different perspective?'

Bronte stood up, uncomfortable with everyone looking at her. 'Well, I mean, if it were *my* tower on fire, then I wouldn't wait for someone to help me. I'd tie the sheets and blankets from my bed together into a long rope, fling it out of the

window, and carefully climb down. I don't know a single princess who wouldn't do that. We're not completely helpless, you know!'

Miss Shine's shining smile widened. 'Indeed you are not. Excellent answer, Bronte. The rest of you, take note.'

As Bronte sat back down, blushing at the compliment, Lance snorted.

'What, from Poop-face? She didn't even answer the

question. Probably because she doesn't think like a knight – she can barely stay on a battle boar, still uses a wooden sword, and believes stupid kids' nursery rhymes about Sir Pen Tine.'

The other boys laughed and Bronte's blush deepened into an embarrassed crimson.

'You may laugh,' Miss Shine said lightly, 'but it's often said that all myths and legends are rooted in truth. Did you know that, according to one version of the Swirklebirkle story, Sir Pen Tine slayed the beast on this very site? Long before it was a school, obviously.'

Bronte forgot about the teasing. 'Really?' she asked in wonder.

'Yes! Although, as I say, that's just one version. There are others too. But it's nice to believe, isn't it?'

Nice? It was amazing! Bronte had never

heard that one before. Just imagine! She could be walking on the same ground as her hero did long ago.

Sir Pen Tine was the courageous kind of knight she longed to be, not the vain posing type like Sir Mallow. Together they would have achieved greatness. He on his battle boar, Hurkle, she on Pig. They would defeat any threat to the kingdoms, and children would sing her name in rhymes too –

'– so if you could write a few paragraphs on that subject, that would be wonderful,' Miss Shine said, pulling Bronte out of her daydream. Now she just had to find out exactly what she was supposed to be writing about!

A Tale of Two Knights

By the next day, there were a dozen ice knights filling the courtyard. Half looked like Sir Mallow, the other half like Sir Ripple. Clearly no students had been given the chance to carve their own.

There was something slightly creepy about the way the ice knights loomed over the students passing by, and Bronte found herself hurrying past quickly. With their ice weapons, they looked like fearsome warriors ready to do battle – unlike their real-life counterparts.

Sir Calliphus had announced in morning assembly that due to the increasingly heavy snow, no carriages could arrive or leave the school site.

'We must all prepare for the possibility of being stuck here for the holidays,' he'd said. 'But never fear, we have plenty of cabbages to keep us full. And we shall begin our winter festivity celebrations today, starting with crown-crafting at lunch time.'

Bronte was so excited – both at the prospect of being snowed in for the holidays, and at being able to participate in some of the school's winter traditions for the first time. Crown-crafting was when the students made a wreath to wear on their heads, formed from the twigs and leaves of whichever tree they were living in. Materials were collected throughout the year and stored safely for this very moment, and Bronte couldn't wait to wear a crown of oak upon her head.

But after they'd eaten lunch, during which Bronte had spent longer than strictly necessary describing her intended crown design, she asked Tonkins what kind of crown he was planning to make, and he shifted uncomfortably.

'Oh, sorry, Bronts, I can't do the crown-crafting. I have a lunchtime club thing.'

Bronte was surprised. Never once had Tonkins had a lunchtime club. The two of them usually liked to take their time enjoying the delicious cakes and sweet treats, going back for seconds and thirds while other students ran off to do activities.

'Don't tell me you've found your voice and want to become a HERO?' she teased. The school choir wasn't exactly very Tonkins.

But his cheeks flushed slightly. 'No,' he said, a little too indignantly. 'I'm a mehfhh.' He mumbled the last word so Bronte couldn't hear it.

'You're a what?'

'A Mallow. I'm a Mallow, all right?' Tonkins said with a defensive edge.

Bronte frowned. 'What the green gravy is a Mallow?'

'We ... um ... support Sir Mallow.'

'And how exactly do you do that?' she asked.

'You know, polish his boots, shine his armour, groom his boar, bring him food –'

'So he's got you doing his chores for him?' Bronte interrupted. 'That doesn't sound very fun.'

'It's more than that,' Tonkins objected. 'Like now, he's going to give us some riding tips.'

'So are you going to the riding arena?'

'Yeah,' Tonkins replied, slightly hesitantly.

'Then I'll come with you,' she said, after a moment. Making a crown wouldn't be as much fun without Tonkins. 'I wouldn't mind getting some tips, seeing as I can't stay on Pig for more than five seconds.'

'Oh, I don't think you can, Bronts. You're not part of the club.'

Bronte pulled a face. 'He can't stop me from standing there. You can always lend me your hat so I fit in.'

His hands flew protectively to his hat. 'This is mine!'

'Relax, I was kidding,' she said. 'But I *am* coming.'

Though Tonkins clearly didn't want her to, Bronte traipsed over to the riding arena with him. Dotty had stayed behind to be close to the fire, and Blue was tunnelling beneath the snow and popping up every now and then, sending snow flurries everywhere.

It was clear as they approached, that all was not well at the riding arena.

A large group of boys, all dressed to look like mini Montford Mallows, were watching on as Sir Mallow and Sir Ripple stood arguing at the fence. Just beyond them, looking highly amused, was Lampton, who was holding the reins of two battle boars. One Bronte recognised as Sir Ripple's champion steed, Guilda the Third, and so the other one must be Sir Mallow's – a fine-looking chestnut boar with his mane all gelled back, just like Sir Mallow's hair.

'It's simply not acceptable!' Sir Ripple was saying. 'I always practise now. Always.'

'And yet, as you can see, I have many young squires gathered to watch *me* practise.' Sir

Mallow grinned, but Bronte could tell he wasn't happy.

'Well, they are welcome to watch me, because it is *I* who will be riding now. Not you.'

'Now, now, Roland, you do not wish to disappoint my young Mallows, do you?'

Sir Ripple stared at the students, as if realising for the first time how they were dressed in the image of his rival. Fury seemed to make him swell in height. 'Sir Double R doesn't move his practice sessions for *anyone!*'

'Well, Sir M&M begs to differ,' Sir Mallow shot back.

'I insist you leave, sir,' Sir Ripple said. 'At once!'

'Never.'

'You will do as I say!'

Sir Mallow arched an eyebrow. 'Oh yes? Who's going to make me?'

Sir Ripple bristled, then reached out and knocked Sir Mallow's hat clean off his head.

The Mallows gasped, as Sir Mallow stared in horror at Sir Ripple.

'It is not honourable to touch another man's hat!' he roared – and leaned forward to tug hard on Sir Ripple's manicured moustache.

'You dastardly fiend!' Sir Ripple cried. 'So it is to be war between us, is it? Very well!' And he ruffled his hand through Sir Mallow's hair, messing it up.

'HOW DARE YOU?!' Sir Mallow shouted. 'Not my *hair*!'

And the two of them fell into a full-blown scuffle, arms flapping as they attempted to ruin the other's look.

Bronte ran over to Lampton, who was watching with a huge smile on his face.

'You have to stop them!' she said.

'Are you kidding?' Lampton replied. 'Right now, they can't boss me around, plus it's far more entertaining than watching them show off in the ring.'

It was hard to argue with that, but Bronte still felt sure this wasn't how knights should behave. It was far from dignified!

Speaking of undignified, Blue was spinning in

circles, chasing his tail and trying to blast it with ice. The icekitten couldn't have been happier, but he wasn't paying attention to the squabbling knights, edging closer and closer to them.

Bronte saw what was going to happen just before it did. She cried out to Blue to stop, but too late! Blue blasted ice, missed his tail completely, and instead hit Sir Mallow on the back of his leg, freezing him to the spot!

'What the –' Sir Mallow cried, as he realised he couldn't move.

'Sorry!' Bronte said, running forward. 'It was an accident!'

'Get that … *monster* away from me!' Sir Mallow shouted, as he managed to shatter the ice and pull his leg free.

Bronte scooped Blue into her arms. 'He's not a monster,' she said defensively.

'Yes, he is! A monster, a miscreant, a menace! I'd wager this weather is entirely his doing.' And Sir Mallow gestured to the deep snow about them.

'It's not Blue's fault!' Bronte cried.

But Sir Mallow was warming to his idea. 'Are you suggesting it's a coincidence that Sir Sebastian's is experiencing such terrible weather right when an icecat shows up?'

'He's just a kitten.' Bronte squeezed Blue tighter.

'Whatever he is, if I see him again, I will be taking matters into my own hands.'

Bronte was too shocked to do anything for a moment. She glanced at Sir Ripple, who was busy readjusting his moustache, and then to Lampton, who gave her a sympathetic smile. Then she turned to the Mallows, searching for Tonkins. He would back her up. Her best friend.

But Tonkins was staring at the ground, seemingly fascinated by a patch of snow he was kicking with his boot.

Bronte couldn't decide whether she wanted to shout or cry. So she did neither. She spun on her heel and stormed away from the riding arena, her cheeks burning with fury. She didn't really care what Sir Mallow thought, or anyone else, but Tonkins not standing up for her?

That was what caused her tears to finally fall.

Quest Survival

When Bronte woke up the next day, the snow was even deeper. Nix, who so far had always been awake and dressed before Bronte, was busy stitching some leather armour on the floor, with a blanket wrapped around her shoulders.

As Bronte stretched and yawned, Nix filled her in on the morning's gossip. 'So the good news is, today's winter festivity craft is garland-making, and then decorating the hall. And all jousting and riding lessons have been cancelled due to the weather, so more free time to do the crafts,' she said.

'And what's the bad news?' Bronte asked.

Nix shuffled uncomfortably. 'Sir Mallow has told everyone that the snow is Blue's fault. He's asking all the students to sign a petition demanding that Sir Calliphus sends Blue away.'

'Sends him where? This is where he belongs,' Bronte said in dismay. 'Honestly, he just hates Blue because he made him slip when he arrived.'

'I'm sure no one will sign it,' Nix said reassuringly. 'But I thought you should know.'

'Thanks,' Bronte replied, grateful to have at least one friend on her side.

'Oh, and there were two bits of Pixie Post for you.' Nix passed her the scrolls. 'Right, got to dash. I promised Sir Ripple I'd help him with some armour repairs before class. I noticed he's been doing it all wrong. See ya!'

Bronte knew she should get ready for the day, but she recognised the writing on both scrolls and wouldn't be able to concentrate until she'd read them.

The first one she opened was from Ellie.

B,

Bad news. We're not going to the Snow Kingdom for the winter festivities any more. Apparently all the snow has started melting! My parents said it was nothing to worry about, but ... Do you remember Aster? Second in line to the Snow Kingdom's throne? Well, she's in Year Six now and she told Lizzie, who told Morgan, who told me, that her kingdom is in real trouble. It isn't just the snow melting, but the icy ground is thawing. All their cold crops will fail if it doesn't get better soon. She's worried that the ice thistle has died, or something. Weird, huh?

I was thinking, now that we don't have plans for the hols any more, shall I ask if we can come and visit you? I'd love to see you!

El x

Bronte's immediate thought was one of excitement that she might get to see Ellie over the holidays. But then she quickly moved on to the more pressing information in the letter: the Snow Kingdom was melting!

Bronte had only visited it once before
Unsurprisingly, given its name, the kingdom was
covered in snow all year round. This was because
of the magic of the ice thistle – the plant guarded
by royalty, which was the beating heart at the
centre of the kingdom. Its icy roots
spread cold through the
land, keeping the ground
at the right temperature
for the frosty crops to
grow. Without it, the
whole kingdom was
in peril!

A knot of anxiety
tightened in her tummy.
A thought niggled in
her head, just out of reach.
Something was very wrong.

Wanting to distract herself, she opened the second scroll.

Tempestra,

I hope this letter finds you well? I fear I'm still unable to return to school. Though my work with the animals is finished, a thorough search of Ackley's lair has led me to believe that mutating the animals was only the first part of his plan to take back the Oak Kingdom. I fear his brothers may still be up to no good, and think it would be best for me to hunt them down before I return. Will explain more when I can.

Stay safe.

Fennel

Bronte reread the note several times. She had met Ackley's brothers once before, in the forest. Elon and Hollis. She thought they had vanished when Ackley was defeated. But clearly not. What had Lady Fennel discovered that meant she needed to catch them? And what danger did she think Bronte was in to use the words *stay safe*?

The niggling thought in her head grew stronger. There was something she was missing – she just couldn't quite think what.

She *did* know that if she didn't get ready for her first lesson, she'd be in trouble, and so she put the scrolls to one side.

Despite everything, she was looking forward to a new lesson on her timetable. Quest Survival Skills absolutely sounded like something she would enjoy. The only downside was that Sir Mallow was taking the class.

'I think you'd better go and spend the morning with Lampton,' Bronte said to Blue. 'We don't want to upset Sir Mallow any more than we have already.'

There was a group of Mallows already gathered at the foot of the triple-trunk oak when she headed out to class. None of them had their firecats in tow – the poor animals were fed up of the cold, and were all choosing to stay inside in the warmth. At least it made Blue's absence less noticeable.

Bronte waited for Tonkins, as she always did, hoping that things would be back to normal between them today. They'd hardly spoken at dinner.

But when Tonkins appeared, also without Dotty, the Mallows waved and called over to him.

Bronte smiled at her friend.

'Hi,' she said when he was closer.

'Um, hi,' he replied awkwardly, shuffling from one foot to the other. 'Listen –'

'Hey, Tonkins, over here!' The Mallows were waving frantically at him.

He glanced anxiously at Bronte, and then at the group. 'The thing is –'

'Come on,' they urged him. And then, to Bronte's surprise, Tonkins offered her one last shrug, abandoned his explanations and turned his back on her as he joined his new friends.

Bronte stung from the inside out, and had to bite her lip to stop it from trembling. He may as well have pushed her into the freezing snow. When the Mallows set off towards class, Bronte had no choice but to trail behind them, very much on the outside.

'His jousting record last month beat Sir Ripple's by two points,' Higgles said excitedly to the other Mallows as they trudged into the forest. 'And he completed the gauntlet run at the last tournament a second quicker than Sir Ripple. He's destroying all the records!'

'Poor Sir Ripple,' Rufus Ranger said.

'Oh, he's just jealous,' Tonkins said, waving an arm. 'And besides, he's always been a bit ridiculous.'

Bronte looked at her friend in his new hat and outfit. Then she looked at how many of the other boys were wearing hats the same as Sir Mallow's. They all seemed a bit ridiculous to her. But she bit her tongue, and kept her thoughts to herself. She didn't want to push Tonkins further away.

It was freezing in the forest, but it looked beautiful – from the white carpet of snow, to the icicles hanging from the bare tree branches. It made her think again of the Snow Kingdom – this was the kind of weather you'd expect there. Not here.

As they stood in a clearing, waiting for Sir Mallow to arrive, a voice whispered, 'Psst.'

Bronte looked at Tonkins. 'Did you say something?'

'No,' he replied, struggling to look her in the eye.

But moments later, the whisper came again. 'Psst!'

Bronte looked around, but no one seemed to want her attention. Huh. Weird.

Lance came striding over, his cronies, Leo and Pole, beside him. He had a scroll in his hand.

'Oi, Snotkins, you haven't signed this,' Lance said, with a smirk.

'What is it?' Tonkins asked.

'A petition, started by Sir Mallow. To get rid of a certain icecat.'

Bronte's ears turned red as her temper flared.

'He's an ice*kitten*, and there's no way he's going anywhere,' Bronte said fiercely.

'We'll see.' Lance grinned. 'It's up to Sir Calliphus, and if there are enough signatures, he won't have a choice. Here – sign it.'

And he pushed it into Tonkins's chest, along with a quill.

'Uh, I . . . um, don't really want to,' Tonkins said, his voice shaking.

'You're a Mallow, aren't you? All Mallows have to sign – it's the rules.' Lance was enjoying this far too much.

'Leave him alone,' Bronte said. 'He's not going to sign your stupid petition.'

'Your choice, Snotkins,' Lance said. 'But if you don't sign it, you're out of the club. And Sir Mallow won't want anything more to do with you.'

Tonkins looked thoroughly miserable as he took the quill and scrawled his name on the scroll.

'Thank you!' Lance said, before shooting Bronte a victorious smile.

Bronte stared at Tonkins in disbelief. How could he side with Lance over her?

She wasn't just upset now, she was furious – too furious to speak. Tonkins did nothing but stare at his feet.

'Good morning, good morning,' Sir Mallow's voice boomed, breaking the tension.

Bronte took a small step away from Tonkins

and tried to focus on the lesson.

Sir Mallow was carrying a travelling bag with him, which he set down in the middle of the clearing.

'Gather round, young squires,' he said, gesturing for them to circle about him. 'When I agreed to come and teach you bright young things, the next generation of knights, I was dismayed that there were no Quest Survival lessons. There weren't when I was a student here either. Upon my departure, I mentioned to Sir Blake, the headmaster at the time, what a vital part of the curriculum it should be. Alas, my advice was ignored then, but now I'm here to right the wrongs! None of you will be unprepared for quests on my watch!'

Despite her dislike of Sir Mallow, and how very unhappy Tonkins had made her, Bronte felt a spark of hope. At last, a practical, useful lesson. Her tummy fluttered with excitement. Maybe they would learn how to forage for food on the road, or what tools were essential to keep their weapons in top condition, or perhaps how to remain hidden when you didn't want to be seen by your enemy.

'Now, let's start with the most important thing,' Sir Mallow said, thrusting his hand into his bag. 'The most essential survival skill I can share.'

He pulled out a little glass jar, filled with a clear substance. Bronte had no idea what it might be.

'Just imagine,' Sir Mallow began, 'you're summoned to a village in trouble. You arrive, dismount from your battle boar, remove your hat and . . . your hair is a mess! The *horror*! Well, don't worry, because that nightmare will never be yours, thanks thanks to Cac-Gel! Made with cactalorian extracts, a plant from the Cactus Kingdom.' And he paused to flash a dramatic smile, staring into the distance.

'Who's he looking at?' Bronte muttered to herself.

Breaking his pose, Sir Mallow returned his attention to the students. 'Luckily for you, I'm an ambassador for this fabulous new product, and it keeps my hair in place, even under a hat. You might have seen me modelling it on the front cover of last month's *Knights Weekly*. Here, why don't you all try some?'

Bronte's shoulders slumped. *Neat hair?* That was his top quest survival tip?! If he was so worried about his hair looking perfect, why wear a hat in the first place?

'**Pssssssstttttt!**'

This time Bronte whipped her head round towards the trees. She definitely hadn't imagined that.

Sir Mallow was busy demonstrating how to apply the gel in an even fashion, using Lance as a model. No one would notice if she wasn't there. And so Bronte slowly stepped away from the class, and crept deeper into the forest.

'Hello?' she whispered. 'Hello?'

'At last! Thundering hooves, I thought you would never hear me, small human!'

Bronte's eyes lit up. 'Lord Errol!'

Lord Errol's Warning

Lord Errol, of the First Battalion of Griffins, clearly did not like the snow. He was wearing a pair of fancy earmuffs instead of his top hat, and had a diamond patterned scarf wrapped around his neck.

'Oh, this stuff is so wretched. Who wants to be simultaneously cold and wet, I ask you?' the griffin lord complained.

'It's so lovely to see you!' Bronte exclaimed, tears springing to her eyes. She so desperately needed a friend right now. 'What are you doing here?'

'Trying to talk to you,' he said. 'But I've had a jolly hard time finding you alone.'

'Are you OK?' Bronte asked, suddenly worried about him. 'Is something wrong?'

'I'm fine, small human,' Lord Errol replied. 'But I'm afraid something *is* wrong.'

A familiar sense of doom settled over Bronte. She knew Lord Errol wouldn't risk coming to see her for no reason, not when humans and griffins distrusted each other so much. 'Is this to do with the Snow Kingdom? Or about Elon and Hollis?'

Lord Errol peered at her over his monocle. 'Ackley's useless brothers? Why should I be here about them?'

'Oh, nothing, just something Lady Fennel said. So, this is about the snow?'

Lord Errol nodded. 'Are you aware that it is only snowing at your school?'

Bronte frowned in confusion. 'What, you mean only in this part of the realm?'

'I *mean*,' Lord Errol said, frustrated with her, 'that beyond the boundaries of this school, there is no snow. None whatsoever. This disgusting cold stuff is only falling here and on the roads around you.'

'That *is* weird,' Bronte said, her frown deepening. 'Why would that happen?'

'I do not know,' Lord Errol admitted. 'But I've spent enough time with you to know that such strange happenings probably require a Tempestra solution. So I shall leave it in your capable hands.'

'WHAT?' Bronte cried. '*I* don't know what's going on!'

'I agree, it is a mystery. One I shall rely on you to solve.' Lord Errol shook the snow from his wings as he stretched them out. 'I simply came to provide you with information.'

'You can't go,' Bronte pleaded. 'If something IS wrong, I'll need your help.'

'You have the cowardly one,' Lord Errol said.

'What, Tonkins? All he cares about right now is his beloved Sir Mallow.'

'And you have the icekitten.' Lord Errol looked about for Blue. 'Or not.'

Bronte sighed. 'It's a long story.'

'Well, I'm afraid *I* cannot help. It is far too cold here for my liking.' Seeing Bronte's disappointed face, he reached out a wing to pat her shoulder. 'Never fear, small human. If there is mischief afoot, I'm certain you will make things right.'

'*How?* Green gravy, where would I even begin?'

Bronte was starting to panic.

'If I recall, last time you wouldn't stop asking endless questions and stuck your nose in everywhere it wasn't wanted. May I suggest repeating such a strategy?' Lord Errol shivered as a clump of snow slid off a branch and landed on his back. 'It's time I went. But I will return in a few days to ensure you are safe. Farewell until then!'

And without waiting for Bronte to say goodbye, Lord Errol soared into the air.

Hurrying back to the lesson before anyone realised she was gone, Bronte thought about what Lord Errol had said. Could there really be something sinister going on? Was the school in danger again?

Green gravy!

She had reached the clearing, and stared in shock at the sight before her.

All the boys now had their hair slicked back in the same style as Sir Mallow, and were practising their best heroic poses.

One thing was for certain, Bronte thought. She couldn't rely on Tonkins to help her investigate the strange goings on this time. But maybe there was someone who could – Nix was smart and capable. If something *was* wrong, Bronte would far rather work with her roommate than alone. Yes, she'd talk to Nix. And something lifted inside Bronte at the mere thought. If the school needed saving, then the two of them wouldn't let it down.

Night-time Visitors

That night, Bronte stayed up late, trying to finish her homework. She was increasingly panicking about it as the days ran out. If she didn't hand everything in by the end of term and pass the assignments, she'd have to redo them when she came back after the winter break, and then she'd fall even further behind . . .

Nix had already been asleep by the time Bronte came back to the room after dinner, and so she was yet to confide in her about Lord Errol's warning. Blue hadn't come back from his day with Lampton, having probably fallen asleep in the cloud shed, so Bronte had her Sir Pen Tine doll beside her for company. She knelt on the floor, listening to Nix gently snoring while she mapped out her family tree. She had gone back many generations thanks to the ledger her mum had sent and was doing her best to neatly lay it out on her scroll.

King Flame

King Duncan

King Prickleton — Queen Esen

Queen Rosalia — King Adad

Queen Flurry — King Torm — Prince Gale

Prince Sturm (Died) — King Tomalin — Queen Thora

Queen Misty — King Mellan

King Cole — Queen Dima — Princess Alya

Queen Mira — King Roy — Prince Perun

Prince Bolt — Prince Flash — Prince Bow — Prince Chaser

The problem was, she couldn't concentrate. She was too busy turning everything over in her head. The strange way snow was falling on the school. The fact that the Snow Kingdom was melting. Ackley's evil plans for the old Tree Kingdoms.

She sat up straight with a start. 'That's it!' she whispered excitedly to Sir Pen Tine. 'It has to be linked!' Ackley had stolen the lightning steeds as part of his plan – what if he'd stolen the ice thistle too? The snow had only arrived at the school after the roads were repaired – Elon and Hollis must have brought it here then! They were probably hiding in the forest somewhere. Which meant that hopefully Lady Fennel would find them before too long and put everything right.

Bronte absently brushed her nose with her quill, until the feather made her sneeze. Ackley was trapped in the skies above the Storm Kingdom, being chased by the thunder trolls. Which meant that he must have given his orders to Elon and Hollis before he was captured. Hopefully that meant that whatever purpose Ackley had for the ice thistle, he couldn't act on it.

But it was still putting the Snow Kingdom at great risk.

'Let's hope that Lady Fennel finds them quickly,' Bronte said to her doll, 'before the Snow Kingdom melts entirely. And before Sir Mallow can get rid of Blue.'

After that, Bronte found it even harder to focus on her work, and it was either very late or very early by the time she finished. She rolled up the scroll, hoping that Sir Calliphus would be happy with what she'd done, and as she did so, something caught her eye outside. A flash of light.

She went to the window and squinted into
the darkness, which was illuminated slightly by
the glow of deep snow. There it was again! In the
distance . . . near the boar pens . . . *Pig!*
It had to be him, his sparkly tusks catching in
the moonlight. He must have broken out again.

The last thing Bronte wanted to do was go
out into the freezing night, but if Pig ate the
cabbages, there really wouldn't be any food left
for the squires!

As quietly as possible, so she didn't disturb
Nix, Bronte pulled on her warmest boots,
wrapped her cloak about her, and then climbed
out of the treehouse.

The school was eerily quiet, everyone else
tucked up in their hammocks and sleeping.
The ice sculptures in the courtyard seemed to be
watching her as she passed, and Bronte was glad

when the moon went behind a bank of clouds,
casting the statues into shadow.

Bronte hopped from foot to foot through
the snow towards the fields where the light
was glowing, gasping from the cold. Honestly,
why did Pig have to be so naughty?

As she grew closer though, she couldn't
see any shadowy silhouettes in the vegetable
patch. In fact, the light seemed to be coming
from further away, up towards the muck heap.
Frowning to herself, Bronte trekked up the hill.
Pig didn't usually come this far.

'Pig!' she called softly. 'Where are you?'

No snort or squeal came in response. She
rounded the muck heap, close now to where she'd
seen the light and –

'Watch . . . where . . .'

Bronte stared in shock at the creature she'd

bumped into. It wasn't alone – there were three of them, and the one she'd walked straight into was the one talking. *Incredibly* slowly.

'. . . you . . . are . . . go . . . ing!'

'I'm sorry,' Bronte said. 'I was looking for . . . well, I think I made a mistake.'

The creatures before her were about the same size as Blue. They had long necks, and crawled on their soft bodies, above which were bright, glowing balls of light. They had long trailing beards, and held walking sticks in each of their little hands. Bronte had never seen anything like them before, but they were clearly the source of the glowing light.

'I'm Bronte,' she said, introducing herself. 'Who are you?'

'I . . . am . . . Hum . . . phrey . . . This . . . is . . . my . . . wife . . . Glen . . . da . . . and . . . our . . .

son . . . Ber . . . tram.'

For a moment, Bronte could only stand and
stare. They all looked the same!

'It's nice to meet you,' she said. 'I hope you don't think me rude for asking, but what are you doing at my school?'

'We ... live ... here ...' Humphrey said, talking as though he had to catch his breath between every word.

'Oh! I'm sorry, I've never seen you before.'

'That's ... be ... cause ... we ... u ... sua ... lly ... live ... un ... der ... ground.'

'*Ohhh!*' Bronte exclaimed, trying to politely ignore how slowly they talked. 'Is that why you have the lights on your back? So you can see?'

'Ex ... act ... ly ... We ... are ... glow- ... crawl ... ers.'

Lampton's story came rushing back to her. '*You're* glow-crawlers? You actually exist? Wow! Does that mean the tunnels under the school are real too? That's where you live?'

'Of . . . course . . . we . . . ex . . . ist.'

'And . . . we . . . did . . . live . . . in . . . the . . . tun . . . nels,' one of the other glow-crawlers said. Bronte thought it might be Glenda. 'Until . . . we . . . were . . . thrown . . . out.'

'Who by?' Bronte asked, surprised. Who knew that the tunnels even existed?

'They . . . were . . . cruel,' Glenda said. 'Told . . . us . . . if . . . we . . . di . . . dn't . . . do . . . as . . . they . . . said . . . they . . . would . . . break . . . our . . . shells.'

'Said . . . they . . . need . . . ed . . . our . . . home . . . for . . . their . . . boss,' Humphrey added.

Bronte's mind was spinning. This was a lot of information to discover in such a short space of time! She had to focus. There were only two people she could think of who might want to hide in the tunnels. Two brothers with a stolen ice thistle, turning this place cold. Two people who she'd heard speak about their 'boss' before. Lady Fennel would never be able to find Elon and Hollis if they were hiding under the school!

'I think I know who they might be,' Bronte said, shivering beneath her cloak. 'And more importantly, someone who can help.'

'Rea...lly?' Humphrey said hopefully. 'You... would...help...us?'

'Of course! First thing in the morning, I'll send a message to Lady Fennel. She's one of the teachers.'

'Thank...you...' Glenda said. 'I...hope... that...cat...is...all...right.'

Bronte looked at her sharply. 'What cat?'

'The...blue...one...' Glenda replied.

Bronte struggled to contain her impatience as the glow-crawler slowly explained that they had passed a stripey blue cat in the tunnels earlier that day and it hadn't come back. She was certain it was Blue. He must have wandered back to the hole to explore. Was it possible that Elon and Hollis had him imprisoned down there? What if they hurt him, like they'd threatened to hurt Humphrey and his family?

'I have to go and find him!' she cried. 'Can you please get a message to someone at the school? At the bottom of the hill are the boar pens, and Lampton sleeps above the feed store. Can you let him know where I am? He'll be very happy to see you.'

'Of . . . course . . .' Humphrey said. 'Be . . . care . . . ful.'

Bronte looked at the hole in the ground. She knew she was being reckless. But she couldn't leave Blue down there alone. She just couldn't.

The hole was a bit too small for her to fit
through, and so Bronte removed her cloak,
crouched down and started pulling at the hard
earth, chunks breaking away in her hands. When
she'd made enough space, she carefully stuck her
head into the hole. It smelled like dirt and trees

mingled with damp. It was surprisingly nice. She managed to slither forward, but the further in she went, the darker it got.

Just as she was regretting ever venturing down, something clasped around her ankle. Bronte screamed, and as she did so, she fell forward, tumbling downwards, and landed with a bump. Seconds later, something – or someone – landed on top of her.

She wriggled hurriedly out from beneath whoever it was and gasped in shock.

'Nix?!'

Underground

Bronte's roommate was scrambling to her feet, looking around in confusion. The light that illuminated the space they found themselves in was coming from the lantern Nix clutched in her hand.

'What are you doing here?' Bronte asked, confused.

'Me? You're the one sneaking out at night and then disappearing down holes!' Nix exclaimed.

'You followed me?'

'Of course I did. I thought you might be in trouble.' Nix looked around. 'And apparently, now we both are.'

It may not have been quite how Bronte planned it, but at last she was able to explain everything to Nix. As quickly as possible, she told her what had happened at the start of term with Ackley and the mutated creatures, how she knew about Elon and Hollis and why she thought they were hiding here with the ice thistle. She described the warnings from Lord Errol, and finished with the most important thing of all – her belief that Blue was down here and likely to be in danger.

'Well, aren't you full of surprises?' Nix said when the tale was told. 'So what's the plan?'

'You mean, you're coming with me?'

'You think I'm going to miss the adventure?'

Nix shook her head. 'No way!'

Bronte smiled widely. She'd known she could count on Nix. For the first time, Bronte had a good look at her surroundings – and gasped with delight.

The entrance might have been tight, but before her – far bigger, and many more than she'd imagined – were tunnels.

'Green gravy!' Bronte exclaimed. 'This is so breezy!'

'Yes, but which way do we go?' Nix asked, holding the lantern up.

Bronte stepped closer to the various tunnel entrances, looking for clues.

'Here!' she called, pointing at the wall. 'A patch of ice. Blue must have left himself a trail to find his way out. What a clever icekitten! Come on, we can follow it.'

It was a good thing Nix had woken up and come after Bronte, because without her lantern, they wouldn't have even been able to see their hands in front of their faces.

The tunnel seemed to go on forever, with many smaller ones forking off at the sides. They followed the ice patches, their route twisting and turning as they ventured deeper.

'I can't believe there's a whole network of tunnels down here,' Nix exclaimed. 'Has Sir Calliphus ever mentioned them in Lore class?'

'No! I only knew about them because Lampton told me. His family seem to have passed down old legends about the school's history. But Lampton definitely thought it was just a story.'

'Wonder what other stories about this place are true,' Nix mused.

Bronte was about to wonder whether the Sir Pen Tine tale set here was true, when she noticed the belt Nix was wearing. It didn't look anything like their usual school uniform.

'What's that?' she asked.

'Oh, this? It's a prototype I've been working on. A belt for tools. But I'm trying to convince Sir Ripple to let me design some new armour that would hold the same things.' Nix patted her hip with a smile.

'That's so breezy!' Bronte said. 'What kind of things do you have in there?'

'A small knife, a slightly bigger one, a little hammer, a chisel, a teeny saw and a mini axe. I made them at my old school a while back. Been working on this idea for ages. Just seemed a good way to always have the practical things you need with you.'

Bronte looked at Nix in awe. 'You're a genius!'

'Well I don't know about that,' Nix said with a smile. 'But I am glad I grabbed it before I followed you out here. Might come in handy!'

After walking a little further down, a glow of light appeared in the distance. Bronte and Nix exchanged glances and slowed to a more cautious pace. They both knew to keep quiet, not wanting to give themselves away.

The end of the tunnel opened into a chamber, which was absolutely freezing. Tree roots of varying sizes pushed through the ceiling and walls, all crusted with diamond-like ice. There were many chests around the room – some bigger ones on the ground, some smaller ones on top of the tables. Lanterns were hanging from the tree roots.

And it was absolutely full of gnomes!

They wore woolly hats, with long knitted scarves wrapped around their necks and draping down their fronts. The scarves weren't so long at the back though, and the gnomes' bare bottoms were exposed, just like the ones Bronte had encountered working in Ackley's lair.

In their mittened hands were shovels and pickaxes, which they were using to dig deeper into the ground.

For a moment, Bronte and Nix just stood there, staring at the gnomes in surprise. And then one spotted them.

'No, don't, please . . .' Bronte begged, knowing what was coming.

But the gnome didn't listen – it started to scream at the top of its lungs!

Once it started, all the gnomes turned to stare. And then they also started screaming.

'Wait!' Bronte cried. 'We don't want to hurt you!'

But the gnomes weren't listening. They started running frantically around the chamber, flinging their tools down and dashing through a door in the far corner of the room.

'Come back! I just want to know what you're doing!' Bronte called after them, but it was too late. They were all gone.

A Discovery

'What, in all the kingdoms, were those?' Nix asked, stunned by the chaos.

'Gnomes,' Bronte sighed. 'They were working for Ackley before, so I think Elon and Hollis must have been here.'

'And I think the ice thistle must be close by,' Nix said, wrapping her arms around herself. 'It's extra-specially freezing.'

'But there's no sign of Blue,' Bronte said, worry hammering at her heart.

'Should we follow the gnomes?' Nix suggested. 'Maybe we'll find him wherever they've gone?'

All Bronte wanted to do was keep searching for her icekitten. But she also knew that she couldn't leave without investigating the chamber. It was too important. With some reluctance, Bronte said, 'No, I think we should look for the ice thistle first. And maybe we can figure out what the gnomes were digging for at the same time.'

Bronte went to the nearest table. It was covered in pieces of paper. There were maps, directions, arrows and question marks.

'What the green gravy could be down here for anyone to find?' she said, confused.

Bronte crouched down to open the largest of the chests below the table. There was no ice thistle inside, but it was filled with scrolls – some unravelled, most still rolled up. She opened one.

It was a very old family tree.

'Hey, look at this,' she said, spreading it out on the table. 'Do you know any of these names?'

Nix joined her and after a while, shook her head. 'No. Never heard of them. Maybe an old Tree Kingdom family?'

Bronte frowned, pointing to a name. 'That sounds so familiar. Where have I seen it before?'

And then she realised. She'd written it earlier that night in her homework. 'I have a distant relative with the same name! Could it be a coincidence?'

Nix pulled a face. 'Mabel Mizzle? It's bad enough one person got called that, let alone two of them!'

'Do you think one of my ancestors married into a Tree Kingdom family?'

'Looks like it,' Nix said. 'But is this important?'

'No, probably not,' Bronte agreed, leaving the family tree on the table. 'OK, keep looking for anything more relevant.'

'Like what?' Nix asked. 'An evil to-do list with the whole villainous plan written out?'

'That would definitely help,' Bronte said with a smile.

They both kept searching, but the chamber was such a mess. They rummaged through the endless chests, looking for any hint of the ice thistle's whereabouts, and rifled through the many piles of parchment – all to no avail.

'Hey, look at this,' Nix said, beckoning Bronte over to the table where she'd been going through some papers. 'There's a whole bunch of Sir Pen Tine stories here. Drawings too.'

'Really?' Bronte asked. 'I didn't realise gnomes were big readers.'

'Yeah, look – here's one about the Swirklebirkle. And how Sir Pen Tine defeated it here on this land. Huh, I haven't seen this version before.'

But Bronte was only half listening to Nix. Because she'd seen something far more worrying. 'Um, have you heard this one before?' She slid the paper over so Nix could see. 'About Sir Pen Tine fighting a weather witch in the Snow Kingdom?'

'No.' Nix frowned. 'I've heard the rhyme about the weather witch, Mo . . .'

'This is different. This one says a weather witch used the power of the ice thistle to bring snowmen to life and create her own army!'

Bronte and Nix looked at each other. 'You don't think –' Nix began.

'That Elon and Hollis are planning to do the same thing?' Bronte finished. 'I think they might be.'

'But these are just stories!' Nix cried.

'So were glow-crawlers. So were tunnels under the school,' Bronte said. 'I think this is it. This is why they brought the ice thistle here. They want to make a snow army to attack the school.'

'OK, let's not panic,' Nix said. 'Firstly, they haven't made any snowmen. And secondly, are either Elon or Hollis a weather witch? And thirdly, why would they even want to attack the school?'

'Because they want to reclaim the Tree Kingdoms. The knights stopped them carrying out the first part of their plan, so it makes sense they'd want to take over the school. Then there'd be no one here to stand in their way.'

'But you said their brother, Ackley, was a prisoner in your kingdom. So maybe this was the old plan, but without Ackley they can't succeed?'

'Yeah, maybe,' Bronte agreed. 'It says in the Sir Pen Tine story that he beat the weather witch by taking the ice thistle and its magic far away, so that the snowmen became lifeless. That's what we have to do, and then it doesn't matter what their plan is. The snow will leave the school and the Snow Kingdom will be saved. We HAVE to find the ice thistle.'

'OK, keep checking the chests,' Nix said. 'There's still plenty we haven't opened.'

Bronte nodded, and frantically lifted lid after lid, until she found a small chest hidden behind a row of others. When she pulled it out, she quickly discovered that it wouldn't open.

'Nix, this one is locked. It has to be in here.'

'Or there's something else important in there,' Nix agreed, coming over. 'Let's see if I have something we can jimmy it open with.'

She pulled a knife out of her toolbelt, and slid the blade into the crack beneath the lid. 'Come on,' she said, wiggling it about. 'Here, try this,' she added, passing Bronte the chisel and hammer. 'Give it a bash at the same time.'

Bronte did as she was told, and the two of them attacked the box until the lid surrendered and flew open.

A snowy blast exploded through the chamber, covering everything with a layer of snow.

'What the soaked sausage just happened?' Nix asked, wiping the snow from her face.

Bronte gazed into the chest with wonder, blinking through ice-crusted lashes. The plant was smaller than she'd imagined – she'd expected something that spread its power through a whole kingdom to be huge. It shimmered silver, with two white spiky flowers, and delicate feathery leaves that entwined with the fragile roots.

The ice thistle.

'We found it!' she exclaimed with a gasp.

'It's beautiful,' Nix whispered.

'You need to take it back to the surface as quickly as possible,' Bronte said. 'Find a teacher and explain to them what's going on.'

'What about you?' Nix asked, confused.

'I'm going to keep looking for Blue. I'll be fine, just get that ice thistle out of here!'

'Oh, you're not going anywhere,' a voice said from behind them, and Bronte's heart sank into her boots.

Ackley's brothers had returned.

Villains

Bronte closed the lid of the chest, and clutched it tightly. But when she stood up to confront the villains, her mouth fell open. One of the brothers was holding Blue roughly in his arms.

She quickly tried to recover herself, standing as tall as a short person could. 'It's over. I have the ice thistle now.'

'Hand over the chest, little girl, and I'll give you the icecat back,' one of them said. Bronte had no idea which one was which.

'Ice*kitten*,' Bronte said, more bravely than she felt. 'And no. We know you're trying to attack the school, but you've failed. Let Blue go.'

'You think we're gonna let you steal what we've already stolen?' The man laughed. 'She thinks we're stupid, Hol.'

'Well, we aren't,' Hollis said. 'And we don't like thieves either.'

'No, Hol, we don't.' Elon narrowed his eyes. 'Last chance, kids. Hand it over.'

'Which one of you is a weather witch?' Nix asked. Bronte was impressed by how calm she sounded.

'You what?' Hollis asked, surprised at her question.

'Well, presumably, for your evil scheme to work, one of you actually needs to be able to harness the magic of the ice thistle, yes?

Otherwise your whole plan is just causing the school some mild inconvenience.'

Hollis and Elon looked at each other. And then they looked back at the girls with suspicion. 'What do you know about weather witches?'

'I know that Sir Pen Tine defeated one,' Bronte said, lunging for one of the gnomes' abandoned shovels with her free hand and holding it up as a weapon. 'And so can we.'

'Yeah, keep back,' Nix added, grabbing another shovel. 'You have a plan?' she whispered.

Bronte hesitated. 'No. You?'

Nix groaned.

'Look,' Bronte said, using the shovel to keep Elon and Hollis at arm's length. 'You've lost. Your brother has already been captured and is trapped with the thunder trolls. You don't have to keep working for him any more.'

Elon laughed. 'Aw, she thinks the boss is out of action, Hol! Well, you're wrong, little girl. The plan is still very much alive.'

Bronte hesitated. Was it possible that Ackley had escaped the lightning steeds and the thunder trolls? Then it hit her! *He* must be a weather witch! It would explain how he had managed to steal both the lightning steeds and the ice thistle – and it would mean he could use his magic to escape his imprisonment to come back here and finish the job he'd started!

'You may as well tell Ackley not to bother,' Bronte said, trying to buy them some time. 'We know you want to attack Sir Sebastian's, just like you wanted to attack POOP and SICK. He's lost the element of surprise.'

'You think you're soooooo smart,' Hollis taunted her. 'You don't know half of what the boss's plan is, or what we're looking for down here. You know nothing about the –'

'Don't tell them!' Elon cried with exasperation. 'It's a *secret* plan, remember?'

'Oh yeah, right,' Hollis said. 'Now give us back our thistle.'

'Give *me* back my icekitten!' Bronte shouted.

'That's enough. No more Mr Nice Guy.' Elon grabbed the other end of the shovel Bronte was holding and started to pull it away from her. He was a lot stronger than she was.

'Here!' Nix cried. 'Catch!'

She threw her shovel to Bronte, who let go of the one Elon was holding to catch it. He stumbled backwards in surprise, completely losing his balance and knocking his head on the wall. Elon gave a little groan of pain and fell on the ground, out for the count.

Hollis stared at her. 'You hurt my brother!' he shouted, and ran at her angrily.

Unfortunately for him, in his haste he wasn't paying attention. He collided with his brother's unconscious body and fell backwards. In the commotion, he loosened his grip on Blue, who took full advantage of the opportunity. He bit Hollis hard and flapped out of his grasp – before blasting him from head to toe in ice.

'Blue! You clever thing!' Bronte cried, as the icekitten flew into her arms. 'I was so worried about you.'

'Hate to interrupt this beautiful moment, but we need to get out of here before they wake up,' Nix said.

'Good idea,' Bronte agreed, putting Blue down so she could use both hands to carry the chest containing the ice thistle.

Together they ran out of the chamber, and back up the tunnels, trying to ignore how out of breath they were getting as they struggled uphill.

'Lampton should already have raised the alarm,' Bronte said between pants as they neared the exit. 'The glow-crawlers were going to tell him what was happening. Hopefully Sir Ripple or Sir Mallow will be able to get the ice thistle back to the Snow Kingdom right away.'

But as they scrambled back out of the hole, not only did they realise that the sun had risen, but that there was no sign of any help coming.

'I don't understand,' Bronte said as they started to run down the hill as fast as they could through deep snow. 'Humphrey said they would go and tell Lampton...'

She trailed off. At the edge of the bottom field, she could see three faint lights. Green gravy, the glow-crawlers really hadn't moved fast!

'Oh no,' she groaned, before shouting, 'Humphrey! Wait up!'

The glow-crawlers came to a stop – though it was hard to tell if they had actually been moving!

'He...llo...a...gain,' Humphrey greeted her. 'And...you...have...a...friend.'

'This is Nix. Nix, this is Humphrey, Glenda and Bertram.'

Nix leaned over and whispered under her breath, 'They all look the same.'

Ignoring her, Bronte asked, 'Have you spoken to Lampton yet?'

'We're . . . on . . . our . . . way,' Humphrey said.

'OK, keep going,' Bronte said. 'We'll go and find a teacher.'

'Sir Ripple is probably doing his early morning dance practice,' Nix said. 'Caught him doing it the other day. I promised I wouldn't say anything, oops!'

'Dance practice?' Bronte shook her head. 'Never mind, let's go!'

But as they made their way towards the school, Bronte caught sight of a figure walking through the snow, and changed direction.

'Miss Shine!' she called out, as she ran towards her.

The new teacher was wrapped in her velvet cloak and smiled at the two girls in confusion. 'Goodness, you're up early!' she exclaimed. 'I don't usually see anyone on my sunrise walks. What have you got there?'

'It's the ice thistle!' Bronte said, and quickly explained everything that had happened in the tunnels. 'We need to get it back to the Snow Kingdom.'

Miss Shine looked shocked. 'You're telling me the *actual* ice thistle is in that chest?'

Bronte nodded.

'And there are two men unconscious beneath the school in secret tunnels?'

When Bronte nodded again, Miss Shine took a moment. She was clearly thinking about how best to proceed. Movement up at the school seemed to help her decide.

'You girls take this up to the courtyard. I passed Sir Mallow and his little gaggle of followers earlier, practising heroic poses. He may be vain, but he is a knight. He'll know what to do.'

Bronte and Nix exchanged a doubtful glance.

'What about you, miss?' Nix asked.

'I'm going to deal with those two buffoons who attacked you.'

'Please be careful,' Bronte said. 'They're

dangerous.'

Miss Shine pulled a sword out from beneath her cloak, and flashed Bronte a smile. 'So am I.'

Bronte and Nix grinned back.

'Now hurry,' Miss Shine said. 'There isn't a moment to lose!'

ATTACK!

As the girls ran back to the courtyard, they came up with a new plan. Bronte would take the ice thistle to Sir Mallow, while Nix would go to Sir Calliphus and raise the alarm.

He'd know what to do to protect the school. It wasn't that they didn't trust Sir Mallow, but . . . actually, no. It was absolutely because they didn't trust Sir Mallow.

Once they'd split up, Bronte sprinted into the courtyard with Blue at her heels, and skidded to a halt at the sight before her.

The Mallows were indeed practising their poses, hands on hips, gazing into the distance. Surrounded as they were by the ice sculptures of Sir Mallow and Sir Ripple, it was a peculiar sight indeed. Then Bronte noticed a familiar face among them. It stung to see Tonkins there. He usually hated getting up early.

Forcing herself to focus, Bronte ran up to Sir Mallow, interrupting their session.

'Sir Mallow! I need your help!'

Sir Mallow preened at the words. '*My* help? But of course.' Then he caught sight of Blue and his smile faded. 'There he is! The wretched creature causing all this chaos!'

'No, it's because the ice thistle is in this chest!' Bronte cried, placing it on the ground. 'It's a long story, sir, but you need to take it back to the Snow Kingdom. Right now!'

'What an elaborate tale for so early in the day!' Sir Mallow said.

'Poop-face probably just had a bad dream.' Lance laughed scornfully. Bronte barely recognised him, dressed up like a Mallow.

'It's not a dream or a story. Please, you need to take it!' Bronte was not only angry, she was tired and angry, which was so much worse.

'Well, I suppose it could make for a good article in *Knights Weekly*,' Sir Mallow mused, looking thoughtfully at the chest.

'What's this?'

Bronte's heart sank as Sir Ripple approached them. Now they'd never get anywhere!

'Did I hear someone say something about *Knights Weekly*?'

'Nothing that concerns you, old man,' Sir Mallow said, the chest forgotten.

'On the contrary, dear fellow, all things related to *Knights Weekly* are of interest to me. I am, after all, their most featured cover model of all time.'

Sir Mallow flared his nostrils. 'I've broken your other records. I will surely break that one too.'

Sir Ripple was outraged. 'You pipsqueak!'

'Has-been!'

'Pretender!'

'Relic!'

'Excuse me!' Bronte shouted. 'Urgent situation here!'

But neither of the knights was paying attention.

A nervous cough behind her made her look round. Tonkins was standing there, attempting to adjust his hat, which seemed stuck to the gloopy gel in his hair. His curls were slicked back and

Bronte realised how much she missed the old Tonkins.

'You don't need to worry,' Tonkins said, trying to calm her. 'I mean, *look*, Bronts! Sir Montford Mallow is here! Nothing, and I mean *nothing*, will go wrong while he's here. He's the bravest knight ever! He's a hero, and now he's *our* hero!'

'Are you sure he's really that heroic?' Bronte asked doubtfully, looking over at the knight who was busy flexing his biceps next to Sir Ripple's as they argued over who had the bigger muscles.

'Trust me, Bronts,' Tonkins said. 'Nothing bad is going to happen!'

A scream pierced the air.

'It MOVED!' someone shouted, and Bronte could see some of the Mallows starting to run. 'It's ALIVE!'

That's when Bronte saw the ice sculpture behind Tonkins slowly raise its ice-sword – aiming right at Tonkins!

Bronte didn't hesitate. She leaped onto her friend, pulling him to the ground before the weapon could strike them.

'What's going on?!' Tonkins cried, as they jumped back up, scrambling away from the attacking ice figure.

Bronte glanced around at the unfolding chaos. *All* the ice sculptures had come to life, and they did *not* seem happy!

'Ackley! He must be here somewhere,' Bronte said, scrambling to reach the chest, and clutching it protectively.

'Ackley? What are you talking about?' Tonkins yelped. 'Isn't he in your kingdom?'

'He's a weather witch, Tonks. I thought he was planning to use snowmen, but his brothers must have told him about the statues. Why didn't I think about that? He's using the magic of the ice thistle to turn the sculptures into his own army to attack the school! They're not ice sculptures any more, they're ice warriors. We have to fight back.' She bent over to scoop up a handful of snow. Quickly shaping it into a ball, she threw it at the ice warrior, hitting it square on the shoulder.

The ice warrior looked down at where the blow had struck and back at Bronte. Then he growled loudly until it grew into a roar!

'Um, Bronts, I think you made it angry,' Tonkins said.

'Yeah, new plan,' she said. 'Run!'

They hurried away from the angry ice warrior, but the courtyard was full of other fearsome statues.

'Why did they have to make so many?' Bronte groaned, trying to figure out how they could get past the ice army.

'Help us!' the Mallows were shouting as they ran around frantically, trying to escape death by ice blade, but unable to make it past the warriors to retreat indoors.

Sir Calliphus appeared at his tower window. He threw it open to watch the mayhem beneath in alarm. Nix was beside him, panting hard from running up so many stairs.

'EVERYONE INSIDE!' he shouted, beckoning for them to run towards the buildings.

But the ice warriors weren't just blocking the way – they started attacking the doors, striking blow after blow on the wood to try and break in.

'Forget that! Secure the castle!' Sir Calliphus cried, disappearing from the window.

'But, sir! What about the Mallows?' Nix called after him, before she too moved away.

'We have to stop the ice warriors breaking inside!' Bronte cried.

'How exactly do you suggest we do that?!' Tonkins shrieked back.

'Draw their attention away. If they're fighting us, they can't get into the school.' And Bronte quickly made a handful of snowballs before launching an attack on the nearest ice warrior.

'Hey!' she shouted. 'Over here!'

The ice warrior glanced in annoyance at the small girl pelting him with snowballs and turned round, his lance raised.

For a moment, Bronte thought he was going to charge at her, but instead icicles began to fire out of the end of his lance.

'**AHHHH!**' Tonkins screamed as he ducked to avoid a sharp stick of ice flying past. 'Why does everything here keep trying to kill us?!'

'We need to take cover,' Bronte said. 'Here, help me make a snow wall. We can attack from behind there.'

As they hurriedly piled the snow higher, Bronte saw some of the other Mallows being chased by an ice-warrior version of Sir Ripple. Lance and his buddies were screaming as they tried to run away, and Bronte called out to them.

'Over here!' she shouted. Lance saw her and changed direction. He and his friends came to join them, quickly helping to build the defence, while Bronte took the opportunity to throw a few more snowballs at the ice warrior pursuing them.

Once they had built a big enough wall, Lance turned to Bronte. 'What now?'

'Now we fire!' she cried. 'Protect the school!'

And together the children began to throw snowball after snowball at the ice warriors.

'Um, Bronts,' Tonkins said nervously. 'You do realise they're all looking at us now, right?'

'Yes, good,' she replied. 'If they're looking at us, they're not breaking into the towers.'

'Yes, but ...'

'They're heading straight for us!' Pole screamed, ducking for cover behind the snow wall.

Bronte gulped, but kept her resolve. 'Keep fighting!'

'Sir Mallow!' Tonkins cried, spotting the teacher trying to sneak past them. 'Help us!'

Sir Mallow stared open mouthed at Bronte and Tonkins and the approaching ice warriors.

And then he turned on his heel and ran away.

'Sir Mallow?' Tonkins said softly, hardly able to believe that his hero had abandoned them.

'Here,' Bronte said to him. 'Just keep making snowballs. We can fight them.'

But as they made a fresh batch of snowballs, the ice warriors fired more icicles at them, and Bronte and Tonkins could do nothing but take cover behind the snow wall.

'Take that!'

Bronte peered out, to see Nix flinging things from the tower window. She was hitting the ice warriors with pinpoint precision, as she threw paperweights, trophies – anything she could find in the headmaster's office – to slow down the attack.

'Stop throwing my things!' Sir Calliphus cried as Nix smashed a chunk off a warrior's arm with an ornament. 'That was my favourite!'

'Sir Ripple!' Bronte shouted, catching sight of her teacher cowering behind a barrel. 'Fight them!'

But as he shook his head, several icicles shot his way, piercing the barrel, and Sir Ripple shrank even further behind it.

'Oh, come on!' Bronte sighed.

The ice warriors were charging at them now, and Bronte wasn't sure they could hold them off much longer.

She hurled another round of snowballs at her enemy, but it wasn't enough, and Bronte braced for impact . . .

Firecats to the Rescue

And then a large black firecat swooped down in front of them and blasted the ice warriors with flames, causing them to roar with frustration.

'Shadow!' Bronte exclaimed, and looked around for the firecat's knight.

There she was! Lady Flora Fennel came galloping into the courtyard on her battle boar, swinging her swords at every evil ice warrior foolish enough to get in her way.

'Where are the firecats?' she shouted at Bronte, as she took in the chaos.

'They're all inside,' Bronte replied, pointing at the building. 'They hate the snow.'

Lady Fennel didn't waste any time taking charge. 'Sir Calliphus!' she shouted up at the headmaster's window. 'Get every firecat out here now! We must protect the students.'

The headteacher disappeared from the

window, as Bronte ran over to her favourite teacher.

'What is happening here, Tempestra?' Lady Fennel asked hurriedly.

'Long story short, the ice thistle is in a chest over there, and Ackley is using its power to make these ice sculptures come to life to attack the school. He's a weather witch as well as an evil scientist, apparently,' Bronte replied.

'Are you on your own out here? Are there no other teachers?'

'Sir Ripple is over there,' Bronte said, pointing to the barrel. 'And Sir Mallow ran away.'

'Sir *Mallow*?' Lady Fennel raised an eyebrow. 'Sir Montford Mallow is teaching here?'

'He's made quite an impression,' Bronte said with a grimace.

'I bet he has. Right then, what's your plan?'

'We need to get the ice thistle out of here. Once its magic is far enough away, the ice warriors will go back to being statues. At least, I think so.'

'Excellent plan. Off you go then.'

Bronte was alarmed. 'Wouldn't it be better if you did it? You can ride out of here on your battle boar.'

'No, I'm going to defend the school. They won't notice you slipping out ... SIR RIPPLE! Get out of there!' Lady Fennel paused. 'Excuse me, Tempestra, I need to save our glorious hero.'

And Lady Fennel charged over to fend off the ice-Sir-Ripple who was trying to spear the real Sir Ripple where he was huddled.

As Bronte ran back to join the others in their little snow defence, the tower windows opened, and out flew the firecats! They swooped down and blasted the ice warriors with fire.

Bronte and the Mallows cheered as the ice warriors began to melt under their attack, while Lady Fennel valiantly fought the ice-Sir-Ripple. Dotty came to land on top of the snow wall, along with Lance, Leo and Pole's firecats too – and together they defended their knights. Blue leaped up to join them, although his blasts of ice weren't quite as effective as their flames. But they were winning the fight!

'Stormy!'

Bronte looked up to where Nix was still defending from the window.

'Here, take this!' she shouted, before hurling something towards Bronte.

Bronte leaped up to catch it. Nix's toolbelt!

'It might be helpful!' Nix yelled, giving Bronte two thumbs up, before renewing her attack on the ice warriors.

Bronte quickly put the toolbelt around her waist, before grabbing the chest.

'I'm going to sneak out of here,' she told Tonkins. 'Get this ice thistle far away.'

'Good luck,' Tonkins said. 'Be safe, Bronts.'

He seemed so genuinely worried for her that, despite everything, she smiled at him. 'You too,' she said, and then crept out from their shelter to try and escape, Blue jumping down to join her.

But they hadn't got far before things changed. Bronte watched with horror as the melting ice warriors began to reform and begin a second wave of attack!

Lady Fennel kicked ice-Sir-Ripple away and leaped back onto her battle boar.

'Firecats, regroup!' she shouted.

While Lady Fennel commanded her firecat army to begin a second wave of defence, Bronte started to run. If the ice warriors couldn't be melted, then the firecats wouldn't be able to defeat them. And she had no idea how long a firecat could keep breathing flames without a rest.

It was up to her now.

The chest was freezing her fingers and it seemed to be getting colder and colder. Bronte wondered if that was because so much of the ice thistle's magic was being used to power the ice warriors.

It was hard to keep running – her tired legs were wobbly like jelly and the cold air was burning her lungs – but she kept going, determined to save everyone.

And then she came to an abrupt halt. Another group of ice warriors were striding towards her, weapons raised, to block her escape.

'When did they build those?' Bronte cried with exasperation. Honestly, if Sir Mallow and Sir Ripple hadn't become so competitive over their ice-sculpting skills, this would never have happened.

She had no idea how she was going to get past the new wave of ice warriors. Blue growled bravely at her side, but it wasn't going to be enough.

The screams from behind her suddenly changed. Not just shouts of fear, but annoyance too. Was that . . . Lampton?

Bronte swung round to see Pig storming through the courtyard. He was thoroughly enjoying his bid for freedom.

'Pig!' Bronte shouted, an idea forming. 'Over here! I have crushed ice, see!'

The pigling heard her, and changed direction,

always keen for one of his favourite snacks, despite the fact that there was snow everywhere!

Bronte took a deep breath as he approached. Her riding skills weren't much to boast about. In fact, she fell off more than she stayed on. But she was all out of other ideas.

When Pig reached her, she gave him a handful of snow to munch.

'I need your help,' she said, scratching his ear. 'I need to get past those ice warriors and out of the school. Can you take me?'

The pigling snorted indifferently.

'I'll give you extra treats for a month,' Bronte promised.

Pig considered it for a moment, and then he lowered his front legs, allowing Bronte to scramble onto his back.

'**Thank youuuuuarrrgghhhh!**' she cried as Pig took off at a full gallop.

She clung on desperately to one of his tufts of hair with her free hand, bouncing up and down as they left Blue behind and ploughed towards the enemy.

The ice warriors raised their swords and lances, and ran to attack Pig. But they were no match for his mighty diamond tusks. He violently swung his head from side to side, using his strong tusks to cut easily through the ice, knocking the ice warriors back and down.

Bronte whooped with delight as Pig fought his way past them and headed towards the entrance of the school. They were going to make it!

And then she lost her balance and went flying over Pig's head, landing in the snow with a thump.

Blizzard!

'Ow!' Bronte cried, as she sat up. But at least she hadn't landed on the chest that had fallen beside her.

Pig had obviously decided not to wait for her, and he was running back to the courtyard. Hopefully he would strike down a few more ice warriors at the same time, Bronte thought.

Besides, she didn't need his help any more. The way was clear. Just a bit further and all this would be over.

She did her best to trudge through the snow, but within minutes, fresh snowflakes began to fall. And they were getting bigger and bigger, until they were almost the size of her hand.

'What the green gravy?' she wondered.

Seconds later the wind arrived, whisking up the snow from the ground to dance with the snowflakes twisting in the air. It kept growing stronger until she could barely keep upright.

The blizzard became so violent that soon Bronte couldn't see anything around her but frantic snowflakes. She couldn't tell which way was out, and raised her hand in front of her face to protect her eyes. The wind howled and whipped up even more.

'Ackley must be trying to stop me from escaping!' Bronte gasped, battling to keep moving. As the blizzard continued to batter her, she feared she was going to be blown away.

Nix's toolbelt! There had to be something in there that could help her. Bronte pulled the small axe out and lodged it hard into the ground as an anchor. Just in time! A ferocious blast of wind struck her legs, and lifted Bronte off her feet.

'**ARRRGGGHHHH!!**'

Bronte cried as she floated upwards, clinging to the axe with one hand, and the chest with the other.

Like a little human kite, she blew around in the strong wind. Nix's axe was the only thing stopping her from disappearing into the sky completely.

And then, from nowhere, a voice called, 'Can I be of any assistance, small human?'

Lord Errol swooped down beside her, his strong wings flapping hard to resist the force of the blizzard.

'Lord Errol!' Bronte cried. 'How are you not blowing away?'

'I am from the First Battalion of Griffins,' he said indignantly. 'You think a little breeze is going to threaten me? Thundering hooves, you offend me. I've a good mind not to rescue you, if that's your attitude.'

'I'm sorry, I didn't mean to insult you!' Bronte shouted. 'I'm impressed! Can you get me out of here? I need to get the ice thistle away from the school!'

With a brisk nod, Lord Errol wrapped his claws around Bronte's shoulders. His grip was firm but didn't hurt, and Bronte appreciated how carefully he was holding her. Then he lowered his head and flew into the blizzard. The wind and snowflakes blustered into them, but the griffin lord was a warrior. He ploughed his way through the storm, heading away from the school.

As he carried Bronte beyond the boundaries of Sir Sebastian's, the wind began to lose its ferocity, and slowly Bronte's surroundings became clear again.

From up high, Bronte could see that there was a very definite line where the snow ended, and normal weather resumed. Lord Errol had been right – the ice thistle's power really had been confined to the school rather than the whole kingdom.

Once they were past the snow, Lord Errol flew for a while longer, until he found a safe place to land. He swooped down and gently set Bronte onto the ground.

'Do you think this will be far enough?' he asked.

'I hope so,' Bronte said. 'I'm not really sure how Ackley is controlling the ice thistle.'

'The wind must have blocked my ears,' Lord Errol said. 'I could have sworn you just said that the scoundrel Ackley was behind all this.'

And so Bronte explained everything that had happened, from the tunnels, to the legends, to Elon and Hollis, and ending with the ice warriors.

'Thundering hooves!' Lord Errol exclaimed when the story was told. 'That villainous scallywag!' But then he frowned. 'What do you suppose the gnomes were digging for?' he asked. 'How does that tie in with their plots and schemes?'

Bronte shook her head. 'Honestly, I have no idea. Maybe –'

But before she could think out loud, the sound of galloping trotters made her look round. Lady Fennel was riding towards them at breakneck speed.

'Well done, Tempestra. The ice sculptures have been vanquished,' she said, as she halted her battle boar beside them. 'Once they became lifeless again, the firecats were finally able to melt them once and for all. The school is safe and so I will take the ice thistle to the Snow Kingdom immediately. It's time it went back where it belonged.'

'Please be careful,' Bronte said. 'Ackley is out there somewhere.'

'If he is foolish enough to follow me, I'll be certain to make him regret it,' Lady Fennel said.

'If you would permit it, big human, I could watch over your journey and keep an eye out for that fiend?' Lord Errol offered.

'Thank you, yes,' Lady Fennel accepted. 'The sooner he's caught, the better. Although his plans to attack all the schools in the realm have failed, so I don't think we have anything more to fear.'

'It's really all over?' Bronte asked, suddenly feeling very weary.

'It really is,' Lady Fennel said, with a smile. 'I won't be back before you leave for the holidays, but I shall see you next term, Tempestra, and everything will be back to normal. For now, you need to rest. You must be exhausted.'

Lord Errol insisted on flying Bronte back to the school before he accompanied Lady Fennel to the Snow Kingdom. As Bronte climbed onto his back, she yawned. Lady Fennel was right, she was tired.

But mostly, she was happy.

She had done it – with help from her friends. Not only had they found the ice thistle and stopped the ice warriors, but Lady Fennel would save the Snow Kingdom while Miss Shine dealt with the evil brothers. Plus, Bronte had ridden Pig and stayed on . . . for longer than usual!

Had she actually managed to end the first term successfully? Could she dare to start calling herself a knight? Maybe even a hero? She closed her eyes and imagined galloping through the kingdoms on Pig, Blue turning the land to winter as they passed – a fearsome team, ready to protect the kingdoms against villainy and . . .

She never finished the thought. She was too busy snoring.

Goodbyes

It didn't take long for the snow to melt away once the ice thistle was gone from the school.

Sir Calliphus declared that after the ice warriors' attack, all lessons for the last day of term would be cancelled. Bronte had no idea how the students celebrated their extra day off – she slept through the whole thing!

The next morning, carriages began to arrive at the school to take people home for the holidays. As Bronte waited for Hopper, her parents' carriage driver, to arrive, she sat in the courtyard with her trunk. The firecats were enjoying the thaw, and were taking the opportunity to bask in the winter sun. Blue, on the other hand, was blasting little snow flurries for himself. He missed the icy weather.

Everyone was excited to be going home – everyone except Bronte. Lady Fennel would reach the Snow Kingdom soon and once it was restored to its normal frozen state, Ellie's family holiday would be back on. And as much as Bronte was looking forward to seeing her mum, dad and brothers, she was going to miss Sir Sebastian's. With everything that had been going on, she hadn't even had time to take part in the winter festivity celebrations.

Bronte spotted Miss Shine coming out of the herbery. Her case was packed and she was wrapped in her velvet cloak. Bronte called out to her, waving as she ran over.

'Miss Shine! What happened? You know, in the tunnels?' She whispered the last bit, in case no one else knew about what had happened below the ground.

Miss Shine glanced around to check she wouldn't be overheard. 'I apprehended those villains, of course! Once I had them restrained, I returned to the school and reported everything to Sir Ripple. He sent for knights from the Deep-Down Dungeon, and they came to take the brothers away.'

Bronte looked at her blankly. 'The what?'

'The Deep-Down Dungeon. You must have heard of it, surely?' When Bronte still appeared clueless, Miss Shine explained. 'Every realm has a dungeon, and this one is no exception. It's a vast pit, with cells in the walls. Impossible to escape from.'

'Oh, I see,' Bronte said, feeling a bit silly for not knowing. 'And what about Ackley? Did they find him too?'

'Why, yes, I believe they did,' Miss Shine said reassuringly. 'You're quite safe now.'

But Bronte was still anxious. 'And what about all the papers? Did you find what Ackley's brothers were looking for? They had a whole bunch of gnomes down there, digging for something. I think it was to do with their evil plans.'

'It was nothing so worrying,' Miss Shine said soothingly. 'They were using the gnomes to create more rooms for them to live in underground. I found the plans among the children's stories – did you know gnomes love a good bedtime story? –

and I think they were hoping to create quite a lair beneath the school.'

'Oh,' Bronte said, feeling even more silly. 'May I at least look through the chests? There was an interesting family tree, and I'd love to read those Sir Pen Tine stories. There were some I'd never heard before.'

'My dear, they've been taken away,' Miss Shine said apologetically.

'By who?' Bronte's disappointment grew.

'Why, the knights from the Deep Down Dungeon, of course. For evidence, you understand.'

'Oh.'

'Chin up, Bronte,' Miss Shine said. 'I can find some Sir Pen Tine stories to share next term if you wish.'

'Yes please!' Bronte smiled at her.

'Good. Now, I must go. Farewell and happy

winter festivities!' Miss Shine sang, waving goodbye.

Bronte watched her go with a smile. How lucky to have found not one, but two amazing teachers to admire.

'Look out, Stormy!' Nix said, before pulling Bronte into a huge hug.

'Are you going now?' Bronte asked, suddenly feeling sad. She was going to miss her new roommate.

'Yep, that's my dad over there.' She gestured to where a man was shaking hands with Sir Calliphus. 'He's just sold some new armour to the school – he gave them a good price.'

'I guess you won't be coming back next term,' Bronte said. 'What with nearly being killed by bad men under the school and everything?'

'Are you kidding me?' Nix grinned widely. 'This

has been the best week ever! I will *definitely* be back. I've got more ideas on how to update my toolbelt after our adventures!'

'Oh, I'm so glad!' Bronte said.

Nix smiled. 'And I've suggested to Sir Calliphus that they put some extra lessons on to help you and me catch up, without us having to lose sleep all the time. What do you think?'

Bronte sighed deeply in relief. 'That sounds amazing.'

'Great. Oh, I've really got to go – my dad's calling me. See you soon, Stormy!' And off Nix dashed, high-fiving some other students from her year as she went.

Someone tapped Bronte on the shoulder. She turned round to see her best friend. And he actually looked like Tonkins again, she noted with relief – gone was the Sir Mallow lookalike hat and outfit. He was dressed in his usual clothes, and his floppy hat with the red feather was back. His curls fell naturally round his face.

'Tonkins! You look like you again!'

He looked a bit embarrassed, as he touched the brim of his hat. 'Yeah, I decided that other look didn't really suit me. Turns out Sir Mallow wasn't who I thought he was.'

'Well, I think you look great,' Bronte said, smiling at him.

Dotty and Blue seemed happy to see each other, snuggling together, their tails entwining.

'Also, um,

I wanted to give you a present.' Tonkins shuffled nervously, before rooting around in his bag.

'What? I thought we agreed not to do winter festivity presents?' Bronte cried, feeling bad that she hadn't got one for Tonkins.

'We did. This is more of an apology present. For not being a very good friend for the past few days. I'm really sorry, Bronts.'

'That's OK,' Bronte said. 'If Sir Pen Tine had turned up, I probably would have been exactly the same.'

'I don't think you would,' he said with a sigh. 'Please, take this.' And Tonkins passed her a package from his bag.

She unfolded the paper to reveal a beautiful festive crown, crafted from twigs and leaves from the triple-trunk oak. It was precisely how she'd imagined hers would look – he must have been listening to her description after all.

'Oh, Tonkins! Thank you! When did you –' she began.

'Yesterday, while you were catching up on some rest. I went and asked Lampton if I could sneak into the store shed and take some bits. Think he only let me because it was for you.'

'I love it so much,' Bronte said, placing it on her head. 'Thank you.'

'I have one too.' He pulled out another crown and took off his hat to make room on his head. 'We can match. And next year, we'll make new ones together.'

'I'd like that,' Bronte said with a smile.

'Oh, and Lampton said to tell you that he met Humphrey and his family and that they've headed home now.'

'That's brilliant,' Bronte said.

'Um, Bronts, who is Humphrey?'

Bronte laughed. 'We have a lot to catch up on,' she said.

Before she could start the story of all that had happened though, a commotion made them look around.

Sir Mallow was striding out of the courtyard, his snooty firecat by his side.

'Don't you know who I am?' he said to no one in particular. 'I am Sir Montford Mallow! I do not need to lower myself to this level. Teaching is for those who can't, and I most certainly can!'

'Looks like Sir Mallow won't be coming back next term then,' Bronte said to Tonkins. They watched Sir Mallow run through the courtyard towards his carriage, as the other students booed.

'Good riddance,' Tonkins said. 'He's not a hero after all.'

'But you are,' Bronte said, giving her friend a big hug. 'It's good to have you back.'

Tonkins blushed a little but smiled. 'Oh, there's my carriage. I'd better hurry. Write to me and tell me everything I missed!'

'I will, I promise.'

'See you next year!' Tonkins said, waving as he ran, with Dotty flying by his side.

Bronte watched him go. Her heart felt full. Yes, she was sad to leave Sir Sebastian's, but what a first term it had been! There had been ups and downs, but she had found where she belonged. It would be nice to go home and enjoy some fun – cloud fights with her brothers, decorating the house with wintry decorations, sneaking into her parents' stables to practise riding battle boars. Maybe by the time she came back, she'd actually be able to stay on Pig, and then maybe he'd behave and not steal everyone's food and –

'Bronte Tempestra!' a familiar voice called.
Bronte searched the crowd, and when she spotted
Hopper, she gave him a happy wave.

'Time to go,' Bronte said to Blue, who was
skating on a patch of his own ice, and she set off
with a skip. She no longer minded leaving.

She'd be back soon.

SIR PEN TINE AND THE WEATHER WITCH MEG

For one of his quests Sir Pen
Tine had to go
Through mountains and
hills to the Kingdom of Snow
The Weather Witch Meg had
turned snowmen to life
Her army was causing the
kingdom much strife

The magic ice thistle was
what gave her power
(It's pretty impressive for
such a small flower)
But Sir Pen Tine knew he
could not fight the weather
To thwart her he'd have to
be even more clever

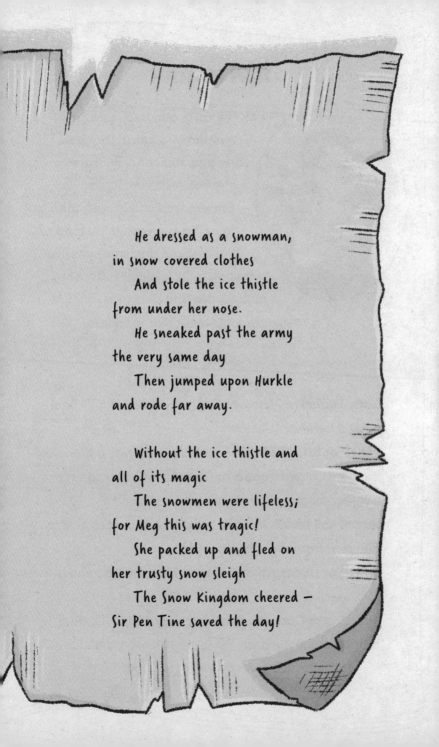

He dressed as a snowman,
in snow covered clothes
    And stole the ice thistle
from under her nose.
    He sneaked past the army
the very same day
    Then jumped upon Hurkle
and rode far away.

    Without the ice thistle and
all of its magic
    The snowmen were lifeless;
for Meg this was tragic!
    She packed up and fled on
her trusty snow sleigh
    The Snow Kingdom cheered —
Sir Pen Tine saved the day!

BEX HOGAN

Bex Hogan graduated from Sir Sebastian's School for Squires long ago, so like Lady Fennel she had to attend in disguise. She enjoyed calligraphy and jousting, but wasn't too fond of mucking out the boar pens. Her firecat, Lula, is black with dusky pink stripes and six wings. Her fire glitters and smells like sparklers.

Lady Fennel or Miss Shine? *It has to be Lady Fennel – what a hero!*

POOP or SICK? *POOP – I would love to ride a pronklet!*

Bare-bottomed gnome or Glow Crawler? *Gnome! I adore their chaotic energy.*

Sword or Mace? *Ooh, a mace perhaps. Just to be a bit different from the other knights!*

Forest or Underground? *Forest. I love being among the trees.*

Jousting or Gauntlet Run? *Jousting. Charging on a battle boar is the best!*

HANNAH MCCAFFERY

Hannah McCaffery was born in the
Sapphire Kingdom, where she
was inspired from a young age
by the dazzling crystal caves.
Skilled with a quill, Hannah
studied at the School for
Prestigious Illustrative
Techniques (or SPIT) in the Realm
of Education, and now works for
royalty and tradesmen alike. She loves
animals, and one day hopes to draw a zombit in its
natural environment.

Firecat or Icecat? *Icecat – I prefer to be cosy!*
Thunder troll or Ice Warrior? *Thunder Troll – I love the
chaos and destruction they cause.*
Sir Ripple or Sir Mallow? *Sir Ripple every single day!*
Storm Kingdom or Snow Kingdom? *Storm Kingdom
so I could see the Lightning Steeds!*
Battle boar or Griffin? *Griffin, far more civilised.*
Crown-crafting or Garland-making? *Crown-crafting!*

Have you read Bronte's first adventure with the lightning steeds?

Bronte Tempestra of the Storm Kingdom will be the first ever princess to become a knight!

But knight school isn't the fun-filled adventure Bronte is expecting - the knights don't seem interested in saving . . . anything. And when she discovers that the lightning steeds have gone missing, leaving the thunder trolls to wreak havoc across the lands, she knows it's her moment to prove just how brave a princess can be.

**Look out for Bronte's next
fun-filled adventure – with the
mysterious weather witch!**

Bronte and the other trainee knights at Sir Sebastian's
visit the Stones of Forgotten Secrets with the
princesses from POOP. But the joint school trip is
plagued by a mysterious mist, which Bronte believes
is the work of a weather witch.

With the camp in danger, it's up to Bronte and her
friends to discover the witch's intentions – a quest that
leads them to question history itself. Can Bronte
succeed like her hero Sir Pen Tine?

We hope you loved your Piccadilly Press book!

For all the latest bookish news, freebies and exclusive
content, sign up to the Piccadilly Press newsletter –
scan the QR code or visit lnk.to/PiccadillyNewsletter

Follow us on social media:

bonnierbooks.co.uk/PiccadillyPress